Thanks to my proofing team, you guys are the best!

Published by Pandahead Publishing, a division of Pandahead Productions. Pandahead Publishing and the pandahead logo are trademark of Pandahead Productions.

Book and cover design by Pandahead Productions

Cover illustration by Tóth "Darbaras" Dávid László

Please visit www.publishing.pandahead.com

The publisher is not responsible for websites (or their content) that are not owned by the publisher.

The characters and situations in this book are fictitious. Any similarity to real persons, living or dead, is coincidental and not intended by the author.

Print ISBN: 978-1-944209-06-3

Ebook ISBN: 978-1-944209-05-6

DEDICATION

A special shout-out to Tom Kater, whose suggestion about title structure made a lot of sense.

I would like to dedicate this novel to my friends. All of them. If I haven't made it clear to you in person, you mean everything to me. Life is much better when you have people with whom to share it.

And a warm dedication to my incredible wife, Allyson. Who also just happens to be my best friend.

-Brett Brooks

a Pussy
Katnip
novel

THE DEVIL WAS GREEN

For five hundred years, the women of the Katnip clan have held a secret. Something passed down from mother to daughter, revealing a ritual which leaves only one woman with the knowledge to create a potion. A magical brew granting the female members of that family increased strength, speed, durability, and healing. It also grants them obscure visions of things yet to come.

In a pact dating back to the origin of the potion, the women have vowed to stand up for the rights of the downtrodden. Fighting against those who would oppress their freedom.

The latest in the line is a young woman who owns a nightclub in the heart of Mutt Town named The Kit Kat Klub. She is also the star performer. But if you have a problem, she might—just might—be able to help.

She calls the potion Fizz.

Her name is Pussy Katnip.

Chapter One

She wanted to get offstage. The song wasn't even halfway over, and it took every ounce of self-control to continue singing.

The notes washed out over dozens of enraptured faces whose life paused just for this moment. Their smiles were everything she wanted to see on any normal night. The face in the sixth row changed everything. The crowd stared up at her on the stage, but she only saw one set of features among them. One very familiar face.

The words kept pouring out of Pussy Katnip by nothing more than rote. And despite that fact, her voice beguiled the crowd like a sailor to a siren. It was her job—her duty in her mind—to keep this crowd entertained. Most of them had come to the Kit Kat Klub just to see her perform, so she couldn't run off on them. Not yet. Not until she finished the performance.

She had no memories of the song being this long before now.

The music swelled. She hit the high note everyone waited for right on cue. Then, the applause kicked in.

A tawny-colored hand surrounded the microphone stand, pulling it close enough to kiss. "Thank you. I hope that you'll stay around for my next performance. In the meantime, the Kit

Kat Klub is proud to bring you the vocal stylings of Miss Jenny Foal."

Pussy took a step backwards away from the microphone before turning her back. By the time she hit the curtain, Jenny was already running towards her.

"What's going on, Miss Katnip? I thought you were gonna do another three songs." Jenny was hopping towards her, pulling a shoe onto her right foot.

"Sorry, Jenny, but something came up. You okay to do this?" Pussy held out her hand, giving Jenny a balancing point.

"You bet, it just kinda took me off guard, y'know." Jenny pulled the elusive shoe onto her foot and then stood up straight. "How do I look?"

"You'll knock 'em dead. Get out there." Pussy winked. Jenny took a step. "And Jenny," Pussy stopped her, "I owe you."

Jenny just smiled and stepped through the curtain. The band hit the first note of her opening song before the cloth came back together. And Pussy made a bee-line for the stairs.

The steps passed beneath her two at a time. She turned straight out into the club when her foot hit the carpeted floor. Jenny's voice was on tonight, and the crowd noticed. She did, too. It was a good distraction for everyone.

The sixth row. Table eighteen, to be precise. She weaved her way to it without pause, and before she arrived the only person at the table was already standing.

Pussy stopped three feet away from her. The other woman stood shorter than Pussy. A delicate white covered her body. Long ears lopped down on either side of her face, peeking out from under a stylish coiffure of platinum blond hair. If you knew where to look, you could see a dark brown patch over her right eye, hidden by a good bit of makeup. Pussy knew exactly where to look.

"Of all the clubs in all the world…." Pussy shook her head. "I never expected to see you here."

"Sorry, Princess," the bunny's voice was soft but clear, "I didn't see a sign telling me to keep out."

"It's been a long time, Spot." Pussy shook her head.

"Six years by my count," the other woman answered.

The song around them filled in the gap. It was something bouncy, talking about the singer's outward appearance. Specifically citing her 'High Highlights.'

Pussy lurched forward and wrapped her arms around the other woman, pulling her into a tight hug. "God, it's good to see you, Coney!"

"I feel the same way, Pussy." She hugged her back with equal vigor.

"Why didn't you tell me you were coming?" Pussy shoved Coney back, putting her at arm's length and getting a better look at her. "I would have taken the night off."

"You still own the joint, right?" Coney raised an eyebrow. "I didn't think you would have to ask permission. Besides, this way it was more of a surprise."

"Come here." Pussy grabbed Coney by the hand and almost dragged her away from the table. With her other hand she waved towards the bartender. A spry young man with a feathered mop of red on the top of his head. He looked over at her, and she held up a single finger, and then pointed to the empty table in the corner surrounded by red ropes. The bartender nodded.

She got to the table and let go of Coney's hand. Rushing to her own chair, she sat down just as Coney settled into the opposite seat.

"You have to tell me what's happened. Where have you been? How are you doing? What's brought you back?" A thousand other questions ran through Pussy's mind, but she held onto them for now.

"Well, let's see…." Coney tapped her finger against her chin, rolling her eyes to the ceiling.

"Oh, stop it!" Pussy laughed. "Just give me the goods! I want to know."

Coney laughed with her. "There's a lot, I guess, but it just doesn't…. I don't want to bore you. I went to Europe, which you know. Met a man, which you don't know. And now…not so much. I'm man-free and back in Mutt Town."

"That's a pretty short version. When did you get back?" Pussy asked.

"A couple of days ago," Coney answered.

"A couple of days? And you just came to see me tonight?" Pussy leaned back. "I'm hurt."

"I didn't want to seem too desperate," Coney laughed again.

Out of the corner of her eye, Pussy saw the man with a shock of red approach with a tray. She stood up to meet him before he got to the table.

"Thank you, Robert." She took the tray and gestured to the table. "I want you to meet someone."

"Sure thing, Miss Katnip." He grabbed the glasses from the tray, putting one down where Pussy was sitting, and the other in front of Coney. Pussy grabbed the bottle and pulled the cork.

"Robert, this is Coney Hase." Pussy poured half a glass in front of the bunny, and then did the same for her glass. "Coney is one of my oldest, dearest friends."

"Really? I never met none of your friends before, Boss." He held out his hand. "Call me Robby. All my friends do. And if you is a friend of Miss Katnip…. How ya doin?"

"I'm doing well, thanks for asking." She held his hand without shaking it.

He responded with a soft whistle. "If you don't mind me saying, Miss Katnip, you got some pretty cute friends."

Pussy tried not to wince.

She saw Coney's shoulders tighten. "I'm sorry, Robby, but I don't really like that term."

"What term?" he asked.

"He didn't mean anything by it, Coney." Pussy held up her glass. "Let's have a toast."

Coney took her own glass and lifted it up. "To old friends."

"To good friends." Pussy remained locked on Coney. "You know, Robert, Coney used to work with me here at the Kit Kat Klub."

"That was a long time ago." Coney let out a small groan.

"Back before I owned the place." She looked to Robby. "She even stayed on after I bought it."

"Were you a singer, Coney?" Robby asked. "Like Miss Katnip?"

Coney almost spit out her drink. "No! You do not want to hear me sing." She chuckled. "We can't all have Pussy's talents. Some of us are just…normal. I was a waitress."

"Don't let her fool you, Robert," Pussy nodded. "She's an amazing woman."

"So," Robby waited until Pussy put down her glass, "is that how you two know each other?"

Pussy shared a glance with her friend. "Not exactly. We met by being in the wrong place at the right time."

"I prefer to think of it as being in the right place at a bad time," Coney countered.

"Well, it wasn't the best place I can think of," Pussy laughed. "But, I suppose considering the circumstances, it wasn't too bad."

Robby's eyes shifted from Pussy to Coney and then back again. "I don't get it."

"When I first came to Mutt Town, I needed a place to stay," Pussy began. "I ended up taking a room in a beat up, derelict building if ever there was one. But it had heart. And it had a great group of people living there." She nodded to her friend. "Coney was one of those people. The best of those people."

"I think it would hurt Joe to hear you say that," Coney turned her head to the side. "I'm just me."

"Joe was like a father, but you were a true friend," Pussy clarified. "I love Joe, but you and I…we were close. We shared things."

Robby turned a chair around and threw one leg over it. He sat down with his hands resting on the back of seat. "This sounds like it's about to get juicy."

"Nothing like that!" Coney chimed in. "We never got into any arguments over a man or anything. I had my taste and she had hers."

"And they never crossed over." Pussy tapped her finger on the table. "Do you remember that one guy? What was his name? Kevin?"

"Kyran?" Coney asked.

"That's him! Oh, what a case he was," she laughed. "I didn't think he was ever going to leave you alone." She turned to Robby. "Just about every day he came by the diner where we worked, and he would sit at the same spot at the counter. He always asked for Coney and then just sat there drinking coffee and eating little bits of food for a couple of hours at least."

"It was worth it. He left big tips," Coney said.

"I bet! The way he kept acting, you would have thought that—"

"What?" Coney interrupted. "That I was selling myself to him?"

"Coney," Pussy recoiled, "that's not what I was saying. I didn't mean anything like that."

"Yeah, well, it sure sounded like it." She tossed her head to the side. Her right ear flopped over, hiding her face as the words faded away.

"No. No, we talked about him all the time. I knew there was nothing like that going on." Pussy extended her hand across the table, resting near Coney's.

"Hey, uh," Robby stood from the chair, "I gotta get back to work. We got a bit of a full house and all."

"Of course, Robert." Pussy looked over at him. "Thank you for bringing us the tray."

"Sure thing, Boss." He brought two fingers to his head in a faux salute. "Nice meeting you, Coney. Hope to see you around." And with that he walked back to the bar.

Pussy turned back to her friend. Coney was looking at her with a blank expression.

"Robert?" Coney asked. "Why Robert? He told me to call him Robby."

"It's a professional thing. Things are different when we're alone." Pussy narrowed her eyes. "Coney, what's wrong? Why did you snap at me like that?"

"I didn't like the implication," she muttered.

"I wasn't implying anything. And you know I know better. I was there, remember?" Pussy explained.

"Sure, I know that." Coney jerked a thumb towards the bar. "He didn't. Why'd you have to go and make it sound like that to him?"

"Sound like what? Coney, I was telling a story. One that, before now, we both used to laugh about all the time." Pussy extended her hand another half inch.

Coney looked down at Pussy's hand, and then pulled her's slightly back. "I just didn't like it, that's all."

"Okay. Okay, I'm sorry. I didn't mean to upset you." Pussy pulled her hand back and smiled. "Let's just forget about it."

Coney grabbed her glass. "Sure. Might as well." She downed the contents. Then she reached for the bottle.

A few replies ran through Pussy's head. She was careful in the one she chose. "What are your plans, Coney? Do you have a place to stay?"

"Yes, I have a place. I'm over on Sycamore, in the old Burroughs Building. I told you I wasn't desperate." Coney took another drink.

Pussy shifted in her chair. She leaned back and rested her arm on the table. "Okay, time to come clean. What's going on? You seemed genuinely happy to see me not five minutes ago, and now you're about as warm as a polar bear in January."

Her hand stayed wrapped around the drink in her hand, but Coney did look up at Pussy. "I'm sorry. I...I really am happy to see you, Pussy. I wanted to come here. Honest. It's just...."

"Just what?" Pussy prodded.

"It's kinda difficult to come in here and see," Coney's head turned as she took a quick look around, "all of this. It's hard to know your friend is a big star when you're as much a...a loser as I am."

"Loser?" Pussy said that a little louder than she intended. "What in the world makes you think something like that?"

"Oh, c'mon, Pussy! It isn't like I came back to Mutt Town because I wanted to!" Coney's voice became noticeably louder. "I came back because I had no choice!"

Pussy opened her mouth to speak, but Coney cut her off.

"That's right. Not all of us are as successful as you are. Not all of us have things handed to us." Coney took another long drink.

9

"Handed to me?" Pussy scooted her chair a little closer. "That's a load of bunk, and you know it! I worked hard to get where I am."

"Ha!" Coney shouted the word in mock laughter. "Sorry, Pussy, but having the owner basically give you a club isn't working for it. Neither is slumming with the poor people just because your rich mom gave you the bum's rush."

Pussy's hand took hold of the bottle on the table, and moved it away from both of them. "Coney, you're always welcome here. That's never going to change. But I think you better get a little more understanding of your stories before you go on about them. Let's leave my mother out of this."

"Yeah, well, she wanted you out of her life, too." Coney emptied her glass. She reached for the bottle. Pussy pulled it further away.

"I think you've had enough."

Coney hesitated, but eventually broke into a laugh. "Yeah. Yeah, you're probably right." She pushed her chair back and stood up. A little too quickly.

As she toppled to the side, Pussy moved to her. She grabbed hold of her arm and stopped Coney from falling to the floor.

"Let go of me!" Coney shouted and yanked her arm away.

"Coney...."

"What are you gonna do, Pussy?" Coney took a step towards Pussy. "You gonna beat me up? Is that gonna make you feel better?"

"Coney, you're making a scene." Pussy could see a large section of the crowd staring at them. "Why don't we—"

10

"Oh. Oh, sure. I would hate for something bad to happen to you! We can't have Pussy Katnip having a bad day, can we?"

"You have no idea what you're talking about, Coney." Pussy stepped between her friend and the crowd. "I have plenty of bad days, trust me."

"Yeah, well, I guess it depends on how you measure them," Coney muttered. "It's probably a bad day when you get called anything less than gorgeous. Me? I get cute. It's always cute."

"It's not an insult, Coney. People say that to you as a compliment," Pussy explained.

"Not to my ears." Her hands flicked her long, hanging ears as if to emphasized the point. "I'm sorry. My CUTE ears."

"Coney, I think you need to go home." Pussy kept her voice as low and calm as she could manage.

"You know what? I think you're right," Coney huffed. "But then, aren't you always?"

Coney spun on her heel and started towards the exit. Pussy fell in right behind her. Just as they reached the far end of the bar, Coney turned back.

"I don't know why I came here. I guess I just wanted to feel like I was somewhere someone wanted me again, but," her voice cracked, "but maybe I don't have one of those anymore. Goodbye, Pussy."

She had already taken several steps before Pussy reacted. "Coney, wait!"

If she heard, she didn't respond. Pussy watched her friend walk up the short set of stairs and down the hall to the exit.

Pussy stood and watched Coney leave. It was all she could do.

"Whew. She pulled a real Jekyll and Hyde there, huh?" Pussy turned her head to see Robby standing beside her. "What the heck was that all about?"

"I have no idea, Robert." Pussy felt her teeth clench together. "But I intend to find out."

Pussy turned and walked up the stairs leading to her office and apartment. She closed the door behind her, and stayed inside for the rest of the night.

Chapter Two

She watched the cab drive away. Pussy considered paying to have him wait outside the building, but this wasn't going to be a quick and easy visit. Not if the previous night was any indication.

There was a small flutter to her heart as she stepped to the door of the building. She shifted her clutch from her left hand to her right. It didn't ease her nerves, but it did help to hide them from anyone watching.

The building had four floors. Six apartments. Names were beside five of those apartments, and none of them were Coney Hase. That left one probable option. Apartment 3b.

The outside door opened easily. She made a mental note about the security of the building as she stepped inside. The age and temperament of the place assaulted her nose. Strong enough to turn her head, but not strong enough to stop her. The first stair let out a loud creak under her weight. The rest of the stairs were less noisy, but she still felt them sink underfoot.

Stepping off onto the third floor, Pussy spotted apartment 3a immediately in front of her. A look further down the hall revealed a second door, and presumably apartment 3b.

Paper and cigarette butts littered the hallway, but at least there was no rotting food or rats. She sidled up to the door, and then paused. A script ran through her head. What she wanted to say. What she wanted to ask. What she hoped to accomplish.

The dull sound of something hitting the floor came through the door.

Pussy knocked on the door a second later. "Coney? Coney are you in there? Are you okay?"

A muffled scream.

Pussy's hand went to the knob of the door. It didn't budge. She put her shoulder into it with no result.

Her hands opened her clutch and found the small bottle inside. The dark red liquid swirled inside as she pulled off the stopper and brought it to her lips.

The world stretched away from her, becoming a long hallway. As it grew in length, images like paintings on the wall moved past her. She saw the silhouette of a woman smoking a cigarette. A box with the number 837 written on the outside. Two dragons stood back to back, their tails tangled together. And a calendar showing the coming Friday circled in red. Then, like a rubber band pulled to the limit, it snapped back. The door was in front of her once more.

Pussy blinked and shook her head. A moment later she put her shoulder into the door a second time. The door exploded off its hinges, falling to the ground in three pieces.

A female figure lay on the ground. She was bruised and beaten, but Pussy recognized her at first glance. Above her stood a man. At least Pussy thought it was a man.

He was tall. Well over seven feet. His skin was alabaster in color, with an obvious rough texture. At the end of his hands were long, curved claws. Similar claws were at the end of his long, three-toed feet. A thick, scaled tail slid back and forth over the floor behind him. Running from the tip of the tail, up his back, and onto his head were a series of raised black spines. Those spines became hundreds of smaller quills, curling back off his head like jagged black hair. Two brilliant yellow eyes stared towards her above his snout. And it looked as though smoke rolled out of his nostrils.

"Get away from her!" Pussy's eyes scanned him again. "Whatever you are."

The monster roared and the quills on his head spread out, making him look even larger. He stepped over Coney and moved towards Pussy. She didn't wait for him to get there.

Her right fist drove into the side of his jaw, turning his head violently to one side. The monster staggered three steps, stunned by the violent punch. Pussy pressed her advantage, moving in and driving her left into the midsection.

This time the creature was ready. Her fist impacted against his hide, stopped cold.

That didn't deter her. She immediately threw two more jabs to his face, driving back his jaw slightly with each one.

The monster snorted. A tiny gout of flame pulsed from its nostrils. And then it roared in Pussy's face.

The claw swiped down from her left. She raised her arm up just in time, but the nails of the monster sliced deep gouges into her flesh. Pussy screamed and jumped backwards. Fast as she was, she wasn't quite quick enough. The other claw raked across her midsection, shredding the middle of her dress and leaving surface cuts across her stomach.

The monster leaped at her, and she met him with an uppercut from her good arm. As he tumbled backwards, Pussy sank to one knee. Her breath was labored. Her right hand went to her midsection and her eyes to the wounds on her left arm.

Her lips pulled back into a sneer. She looked back up just in time to see the creature regaining his feet.

"What are you?" she snarled.

It hissed in response and fell into a crouch. A second later it jumped towards the window.

The glass shattered as he went through. Pussy was up and sprinting to it before the last shard hit the ground. The creature was already down the fire escape outside the window.

"No you don't." Pussy climbed out the window and moved to the outside of the railing. She let go and dropped down one flight, catching the railing there. One more drop put her on the ground.

Instinct told her to move, and she listened. She rolled off to the side, keeping low to the ground. A garbage can rang off the wall and clattered to the middle of the alleyway.

She sprang to her feet. The creature had already hefted another garbage can above his head. Pussy ran towards him, side stepping the second garbage can he threw her way.

The first thought of punching the monster was pushed aside, and Pussy chose a different approach. She launched herself, driving her right shoulder into him. The creature was thrown back into the wall with all the power Pussy could muster.

She felt the air leave its lungs, so she pulled her shoulder back and thrust it into his midsection a second time. His body slumped slightly, but he was still standing.

And then she felt the claws digging into her back. Pain shot through her and the sound of tearing cloth filled her ears. She had no choice. Dropping down, she rolled off to the side again. Her legs propelled her back up, but the sharp pain in her back held her in place for the moment.

His chest swelled as it filled with air. She took the same time to collect herself. And she noticed that his chest was still rising.

He opened his mouth, spewing out a gout of fire. She sprung to the side, leaping for one of the garbage cans he had thrown at her. The fire singed the end of her tail as she tucked in behind the metal canister. The heat was intense, but the core of the attack missed her. The garbage can wasn't much, but it was enough to deflect the flame.

She waited a second after the blazing attack ended before she dared to show her head. The creature had already made it halfway up the building across the alley. Only this one had no fire escape.

It's claws dug into the brick with every move. Faster than Pussy thought possible, it scampered up the wall and moved over the edge and out of view.

"Another time, then," she muttered.

The pain hit her hard. She looked down at her stomach. The healing aspect of the Fizz had almost closed those shallow wounds. The deeper cuts on her arm and back would take more time. Time she couldn't wait to pass.

Leaping up, she grabbed hold of the fire escape ladder and pulled herself back onto it. The stairs passed underneath her as the image of Coney on the floor came back to her.

When she reached the window, the picture hadn't changed. Coney was in the exact position as when Pussy left. Her left eye was swollen to the point where it was almost closed. Her mouth was a mess of cuts and bruises, though no blood was visible.

Pussy scrambled back inside and ran over to her friend. She was still, and a cold feeling jolted up Pussy's spine.

"Coney?" Pussy whispered. "Can you hear me?"

Nothing. She felt her eyes grown damp.

"Coney!" Pussy grabbed ahold of her friend by the shoulders and shook her.

The brown patch on Coney's face was clear. No makeup. And the eye in the middle of it opened a crack.

"Coney!" Pussy shouted again.

She saw her friend's right hand move, lifting a couple of inches off the floor. Coney's mouth opened, and a faint garbled sound escaped. Pussy took hold of her friend's hand.

"It's okay. Don't worry, I'll call an ambulance. We'll get you to the hospital. Everything is going to be fine." The tears rolled down Pussy's cheeks. Something cold pressed into the palm of Pussy's hand.

And then Coney went completely limp.

"Coney?" Pussy shook her friend again. Her voice broke. "Spot?"

She cradled Coney's head against her. When she let go of Coney's hand, Pussy felt cold travel with her, trailing off her hand.

In the palm of her hand was a necklace. A pendant with an abstract shape on a silver chain. A curling line the swept up and then back down. Another line crossed over it and ended in a curl. She recognized it. Coney wore that necklace since Pussy had first met her.

Coney said it was a symbol of eternal friendship.

She let the chain drop down to it's full length, until the pendant dangled in front of her. Her jaw clenched tight, and she felt her eyes squeeze the last of the tears out. Carefully moving Coney, she placed her head back on the ground. Blood from the deep wound on Pussy's arm stained the white fur on the side of Coney's face.

"I'm going to find who did this, Coney," Pussy growled. "I swear I'll find them, and I'll make them pay."

"Don't move!"

Pussy jumped to her feet and spun around, ready for the worst.

Three policemen stood in the doorway, nightsticks in hand. "Don't move!" the one in the front repeated. "Get down on the ground!"

She lowered her arms. "It's not what it looks like. I found her like this."

"I'm not gonna tell you again, lady," the officer shouted, "get down on the ground."

"That's her, officers!" A voice shouted from behind them. Pussy glanced up to see a mousy young woman pointing at her. "She's the one who busted in the door. I saw it."

Two more officers appeared in the hallway. Pussy began to weigh her options.

"I didn't do this. She's…she was my friend." Pussy took a step back away from Coney.

"Put your hands up!" A different officer commanded.

"Get on the ground!" The first one repeated.

The images from earlier flashed through Pussy's head. The number 837. Two dragons with their tails entwined. The circled day. Friday. Only three days away. Her fist closed on the necklace.

"I can't do that, officers." She took another step backwards. "I can't take that chance. I have to be free for the next three days."

"Don't do anything stupid, lady," two of the policemen moved into the room. "We've got you surrounded."

She looked at Coney's body. The words of the previous night echoed in her head. Harsh words. Angry words. The last words they ever spoke to each other.

"I'm sorry."

Pussy dashed to the window and jumped through it. Her hand caught hold of the railing and flipped her over it. She barely took time to stop on the level below. Springing off of the railing, she propelled herself towards the back of the alley.

Her feet moved like lightning. The sound of policemen shouting faded in her ears until they were completely gone.

But she didn't stop. She couldn't stop. All she could do was run. With every step her eyes drew tighter, and her resolve grew stronger.

Chapter Three

She crushed out her cigarette and then lit another.

"Ringtail!"

The smoke poured from her mouth as much as she pushed it out. She put the cigarette in the corner of her lips and walked into the room. A handful of men still wandered about. One was taking pictures. One was gathering potential evidence. Two stood to the side, watching everything. And the final one was already annoying the hell out of her.

"Nice to see you, too." Her voice carried a bit of a rough edge as she headed towards the side bedroom where he waited.

"Nice of you to finally show up. This is supposed to be your case, remember?" He was a short pig of a man. His uniform was ill-fitting and his manners less so. The few strands of what he called hair on his head were black, and amazingly dirty all things considered. "You need to start acting like it."

She was a stark contrast to him. Though most wouldn't consider her tall, she still seemed to tower over him. Her suit was immaculate, matching the rest of her appearance. The gray-brown hair she pulled back into a tight bun behind her head was clean and slick. And her cool gray eyes shined out from the tell-tale mask surrounding them. "Why Officer Stye, you seem upset. Is anything wrong?"

"Can it, Ringtail. The lieutenant wanted me here, but I don't have to like it." He jerked his thick thumb over towards a young woman huddled into a chair. "Like I said, this is your case. This dame has info for you."

The girl was shaking. She pulled her knees up to her chest and her whole body rocked in the chair.

"Yeah. Yeah, I got it, Stye," she sighed. "Why don't you go get a glass of water for our guest."

He snorted, but said nothing and walked out of the room. Presumably to get the requested water.

She kneeled down in front of the woman and pulled the cigarette from her mouth. "Hi there. I'm Detective Lila Ringtail. What's your name?"

The woman wasn't much younger than Lila, if at all. She looked up and sniffled. "Muri."

"Can you tell me what happened here, Muri?"

The mousy woman nodded. "There was this woman. I didn't see her come into the building, but I heard her in the hallway. She was banging on the door. It was really loud. I was trying to listen to the radio, you know? My soap was on, and it was really distracting." She sniffled again. "So, you know, I went outside and there she was. She ran through the door like it was paper. It just exploded, you know? So, I came back inside and I called the police."

"Did you see anything else, Muri?" Lila kept her voice soft and low.

She shook her head. "No. Not really. I started to walk down the hall, and that's when I heard something happening. A fight or something, you know? It was loud and…and I thought I heard something roar in there. So, I just kinda ran back into my apartment."

"A roar?" Lila pressed.

"Yeah. I mean, I've never actually heard a roar, but that's how they sound on the radio. On those shows that have lions on them and stuff, you know?" She let go of her legs and lowered her feet to the floor.

"Is there anything else? Anything at all? It could be important."

"I'm sorry." Muri's sniffle was softer. "Is…did that woman…is she, you know, dead?"

"I'm afraid so, Muri. How well did you know her?" Lila asked.

"I didn't. She just moved in a couple weeks ago, you know? I never even got her name. Cute kid. Always smiled at me in the hallway. Seemed like a really nice gal."

The officer walked back in carrying a glass of water. Lila stood back up and returned the cigarette to the corner of her mouth. "Stye, why don't you take Muri back over to her apartment. Get her information so we have it." Lila looked back down at the woman. "Are you okay with that, Muri?"

She nodded in reply.

"I'm not supposed to leave you alone," Stye answered. "The lieutenant—"

"The lieutenant ain't here. Get her back home. I'm not going anywhere, and you can come back over and glare at me when you're done." Lila raised her eyebrows. "Or is that too tough for you?"

Lila could almost see the steam coming out of his ears. "C'mon, lady." He stomped towards the door. "Let's get you back to your place. This one is starting to smell bad anyway."

She pulled the cigarette from her mouth, and a long stream of smoke blew out onto Stye's face.

He did his best not to cough. She didn't even attempt to hide her smile.

Stye led Muri out of the room and then the apartment. Lila stepped out of the room and back into the living area where they found the body. The photographer was packing up his stuff.

"You get everything?" she asked him.

"As much as I could," he replied.

"Do me a favor and get a copy of everything, would ya?" she asked. "When do you think you'll have them?"

"Gotta get back to the precinct, and then the lab...." His voice trailed off. "Maybe today. If not, tomorrow morning."

"Today's better. Do what you can." She put out her hand. "Thanks."

He looked down at the hand. For two seconds he stared at it, and then moved his eyes up to hers. Then he turned and headed towards the door. "Just doing my job."

She didn't watch him leave the room. Instead, she turned and knelt down beside the body. A young woman of lagomorph heritage. Visible trauma was clear on her face. Particularly around one eye and her mouth. The only blood was on the side of her face, away from the trauma. A red splotch that faded to pink around the edges.

Lila picked up the dead woman's hands and examined them. First the left, and then the right. Each time she set them back directly where they initially laid.

She stood up and pulled the cigarette from her mouth. A long trail of ash hung from the tip. Scanning the room, she saw no ashtrays. So she tipped them off into her hand and then dropped them into her pocket.

The floor around the body was mostly clean. A few specks of blood here and there. A few feet away a large spattering stained the carpet. Then a few trickles carried throughout the room.

Lila walked over to the window. One of the officers was dusting the sill for fingerprints.

"Anything?" she asked.

"Yeah. Lots, actually. Too many. Just a big mess of prints. Nothing clean," he stated.

"No surprise. Kind of a waste of time if you ask me." Lila craned her head and stared beyond the window. Shards of glass littered the fire escape.

"Well, the lieutenant said to dust, so, I'm dusting." He went right back to work.

"Do you mind?" She pressed forward, hinting for him to move to one side. He stepped to his right.

She leaned out of the window, looking at the glass. Clean shards of glass scattered all the way to the edge of the platform. She pulled herself back inside.

"Anybody been down below?" Lila asked.

"I don't know," the officer answered.

"Okay, well, then stop what you're doing and go down to that alley. Let me know if you see any blood down there." She pointed out the window.

"I'm supposed to look for prints," he responded.

"Okay. Then go look for prints down in the alley. And while you're down there, do me a favor and see if there's any blood." She took the cigarette out of her mouth and tapped the ashes outside the window.

"I'm not—"

"Do it!" Any hint of request was gone. This was an order.

The officer put the dust and brush back into the small bag next to the window. He gathered it up and stepped out onto the fire escape. A low mumble reached Lila's ears.

"Didn't quite catch that," she said.

His mouth barely moved as he spoke. "I said, yes ma'am."

"I'm sure," she answered. "Thank you."

She turned back to the interior of the apartment. The furniture—what little there was of it—was pushed around. Definite sign of a struggle. No furniture was anywhere near the body.

Lila walked to the kitchen. A coffee mug was in the sink. Nothing else was visible, so she began opening drawers. Each one came up the same. Empty. A trip to the refrigerator revealed a bottle of milk and a white bag. A look inside revealed a half-eaten piece of carrot cake. Nothing else.

As she walked back into the main room, Officer Stye did the same.

"I got her back to her place," he grumbled.

"Good," Lila answered. "Now, tell me why the hell she was here to begin with?"

"What? She was a witness. She needed—"

"She needed to not be in the middle of the crime scene. There's a dead body, in case you forgot. That girl was scared half out of her wits. I never thought of you as a genius, Stye, but I didn't think you were that stupid, either."

"Hey! You were the one who was late. If you—"

"Sell it walking, Stye." She stepped over to the bedroom where they questioned the young woman. The bed was made. A lamp on the side table. She walked to the dresser and pulled open the top drawer. A selection of women's undergarments were scattered around. The four drawers below it were empty.

The closet in the room held a half-dozen dresses. Nice ones. Lila checked the labels and couldn't read a word on any of them. Four pairs of shoes sat in a row on the closet floor.

"What are you doing?" Stye asked.

She looked over her shoulder at him. "Looking in the closet."

He snorted. "I can see that."

"Nothing gets past you." She closed the closet and walked back to the door. Stye stepped aside and she went past him and to the only room left in the apartment.

The bathroom was spartan. A sink, a toilet, and a bathtub. She opened the medicine chest. A toothbrush and some polishing powder. A bottle of aspirin. And another bottle of pills without a label. Lila picked up the unlabeled bottle.

"You shopping for a new place to stay?" Stye asked.

"Will it get me further away from you?" she replied.

31

"The stiff's out here, ya dumb broad." The volume of his mumble was just loud enough to carry to her ears.

Lila kept the bottle of pills and closed the medicine cabinet. "Did you talk to the manager of the place yet?"

"We called him, but he hasn't shown up." Stye was standing next to the body. She walked past him and back to the window.

Carefully, she stepped through the broken window and moved onto the fire escape. The officer was standing over near the building on the other side of the alley.

"Anything?" Lila called down.

He turned and looked up at her. "Yeah. There's a lot of blood over here."

Lila glanced over to her right. A red spot was on the iron railing. "Thanks. See if you can't get a sample of it." She pulled the cigarette out of her mouth and tapped off the ashes.

As she stepped back through the window, Stye was already talking. "Gonna take some time to look at the body now?"

"I already did," Lila answered. "She's dead."

"You're a ditzy dame, you know that?" Stye grumbled. "It don't matter, I suppose. We know what happened. We just gotta find the broad who did it."

"Why?" Lila asked.

"Because she killed this here woman." Stye pointed to the ground.

"No." Lila shook her head. "Why'd she go out that window, then come back inside?"

"What do you mean?" Stye stepped over to her.

"We have an eye witness who saw this woman bust down the door. Then four officers caught her in the act." Lila looked out the window. "But our dead friend isn't cut. Badly bruised, but not cut. And that window was busted out before the cops got here. There's blood outside. So, it looks like the woman we're looking for was bleeding, went outside, and then came back in." She looked at Stye. "Why?"

"I don't know. How can you be sure she did? Maybe that window was already busted. And if she was bleeding then she just got it out there when she ran," Stye suggested.

Lila took a deep drag off her cigarette and blew the smoke out her nose. "No. I was told that the officers gave chase. She wouldn't have had time to leave the blood in that area of the alley."

"Well maybe she just bleeds a lot." Stye groaned. "How the heck are we supposed to know?"

"We aren't," Lila answered. "I am."

"Detective." The other officer stepped forward. There was something in his hand. "I found this under that chair." He pointed to an overturned wing chair in the corner.

He held out a small gold clutch purse.

Lila took it. She turned it over once, and then opened it. Her hand went inside and pulled out a small bottle. Holding it up to the light, she saw a thin coat of red liquid on the bottom of it. She went back to the clutch, looking as she dug around. Her hand came to a stop.

"Huh."

With two fingers she pulled out a matchbook. It was black with silver letters on the cover. The words read "Kit Kat Klub."

Lila turned and started towards the door.

"Where are you going?" Stye asked.

She held up the match book.

He scampered after her. "Oh no you don't. The lieutenant won't want you poking your nose around without someone else there."

"Oh good. More time together." She crushed out her cigarette and then lit another.

Chapter Four

She heard the door close. More importantly, she heard the conversation that followed. Pussy went right back to the bottles and her task at hand.

It wasn't long before they made their way into the room.

"Hey, Miss Katnip." Robin's voice was as bouncy as her step. "What ya' doin'? Need help? I can grab some goods if you want. I got nothing going right now."

It wasn't anything new. Robin had been crushing on her for a while now. Pussy found it flattering, if not a little strange. "I'm almost done, actually." She glanced up at Robin and her brother Robby walking just behind. "I'm glad you're here, though. We need to talk."

"That kinda tone gets my gas going the wrong way." Robby walked to the bar. "What's the deal, Miss Katnip?"

She went back to work. Pussy's hands steadily poured from bottle to vial. "I went to Coney's place this morning, and—" Her hand lurched. The Fizz spilled out across the counter, splashing up onto her arm. She set the bottle down.

"Pussy?" Robby's voice was soft, with more than a hint of tension beneath it. "What's wrong?"

She looked up again. Robby looked angry. Robin looked terrified. "Coney's dead." The words forced tears from the corners of her eyes.

"Oh no," Robby whispered.

"I didn't...." Robin's eyes danced back and forth between the two. "Who...who's Coney?"

"I'll explain later," Robby answered. "Pussy, what happened?"

She measured her words before she spoke. "A dragon killed her."

Robin snorted. "What? You're joking." She looked at her brother. "She's joking."

"I don't think so," Robby muttered.

"Trust me, I know how it sounds. I wouldn't have believed it if I hadn't seen it myself." Pussy gathered the filled vials together. Six of them run to the top with Fizz. She pressed in a cork to cap off each one. "I can't really explain it, but I do know what I saw. And the only term I can think of to describe it is dragon."

They stared at her. Robin's mouth hung slack. Robby just stayed silent.

"There's more."

"How much more?" Robby asked.

She put the vials in the pockets of her robe. After tightening her belt, Pussy went around to the other side of the bar. She stood beside the siblings. "The police are going to come here.

They are going to be looking for me, and they are going to tell you that I killed her." She felt her jaw clench. "I didn't. I tried to save her."

"Wh-why would they think that?" Robin whispered.

She did her best to smile. It occurred to her that it might look like a snarl, so she stopped. "The neighbor heard what was going on and called them. When they got there I was holding Coney's body. Blood was all over the both of us."

"Oh no." Robby stepped towards her. "Don't worry. The buttons can come here and ask whatever they want. We know the truth and we'll tell them to their face. We'll get this cleared up."

"No." Pussy interjected. "You can't let them know I was here. That will just cause more of a mess."

"If we don't tell them, they'll keep looking for you. You'll be a hood. An actual criminal. If you turn up they'll understand. Everyone gets scared, Pussy. Even you."

"I have to, Robby. I have three days to find her killer." Pussy shook her head. "And don't ask me how I know that. I just do. If I go with the police there is a chance they'll hold me for a few days while things clear up. I can't take that chance."

"You gotta!" Robby pleaded. "Pussy, they'll throw you in the hoosegow. For good."

She looked him in the eye. "If it was Robin, what would you do?"

"I…." He couldn't go any further.

"Coney was like a sister to me. She was the only family I had before I got the club," Pussy said.

"And now you have us," Robby answered. "We're family too, right?"

"You know you are." Pussy knew where this was going. "There isn't a chance that you won't see me again, Robby. And even if something does happen to me, I've got things in place to take care of you, Robin, Jenny, and everyone here."

"You can take care of us by being here," Robby insisted.

"Robby, I'll be back. This is my club. My home. One way or another I'm coming back to it. And I promise to turn myself over to the police." She tried to force the smile again. "It will work out."

His face contorted. She saw all the things he wanted to say reflected in the way his mouth twitched. They stayed inside. "It better."

"Thank you," Pussy whispered. She turned to Robin. "Can you help me with something up in my room? It shouldn't take too long."

"Me?" Robin pointed to herself. Her eyes lit up. "Sure. Yeah, I'd be happy to help out."

"Thanks." Pussy started towards the stairs, but took a second to speak over her shoulder as she went. "We'll be right back, Robby. Then we can go over anything else before I head out."

Robby just nodded. Pussy walked up the stairs to her apartment, with Robin right on her heels. They walked inside and Robin shut the door behind her.

"I appreciate you doing this, Robin." Pussy began to loosen her robe. "I had a few minutes before you and Robby arrived, so I was able to handle some of it, but the rest…." She lowered the robe off her shoulders.

Robin stared at her, mouth agape. All Pussy was wearing was her undergarments. Pussy turned around and put her back towards the young woman.

She heard Robin gasp. "What happened?"

"That dragon I was talking about." Pussy glanced over her shoulder. "He got my arm as well, but I was able to bandage that. I was hoping you could help me with—"

"Pussy, you need to see a doctor!" Robin ran her fingers along the edge of the wound. "This looks bad."

"I'll be fine, Robin. I just need you to put some bandages on it for me. I don't want anything getting into the wounds." Pussy pointed over to a nearby table. Everything was already waiting. "There's some alcohol and gauze over there. Clean the wound and put the gauze on it, and that's it."

She hesitated, but Robin went to the table. "Come over here, it'll be easier."

Pussy walked up to her and turned her back again.

"I don't know how you can do this," Robin muttered. "This isn't the first time you've been hurt. Why do you keep getting yourself hurt?"

She didn't turn around. "Because if I don't, someone else will."

"That doesn't make any sense."

Pussy winced as the alcohol hit the wounds. "It's hard to explain, Robin. A long story. Suffice it to say that I've got an obligation."

"That's a load of bunk if you ask me."

"Even if I agreed with you, I would still do it in this case." The volume of her voice dropped a few levels. "I owe it to Coney."

Robin worked in silence. Pussy felt her lay the gauze and tape it in place. Finally, she spoke. "How…close were you and Coney?"

"I wasn't joking, Robin. She was like a sister to me. When we first met, neither one of us had anything. We sort of found it together." Pussy's mind wandered back several years. "I guess you could say I grew up with her."

"So, friends then?" Robin asked.

Robin took a step back, putting the remainder of the gauze back on the table. Pussy turned to face her.

"Not typical friends. We were much closer than that, but yes, just friends." Pussy made her way towards the bedroom. "I remember one time, shortly after we met, that she and I went out to a club. A real dive. But the booze was cheap and that fit our budget perfectly."

Pussy walked to her closet. Robin leaned against the doorway of the bedroom. Pussy opened the closet up and started rummaging through clothes. "Anyway, we were there, minding our own business, when these three guys came up and started in on us. Not very smooth, either. A lot of the girls there were real chippy, so I guess I couldn't blame them, but they just didn't take no for an answer."

"So you had to do something about it?" Robin asked.

Pussy laughed. "No. I probably would have, but Coney handled it all herself. She looked up at these guys and, in a really loud voice, said, 'Do you want to hear a joke about my body?' Naturally, they said yes. She smiled and said, 'Never mind.

You'll never get it.' Everyone around us busted out laughing. The three men walked off with red faces."

Robin chuckled. Pussy slipped into a skirt and zipped it closed.

"That's Coney. I've never known anyone who was as quick-witted as her. She always knew what to say and what to do." She pulled a shirt on, and then sat down on the bed to put on some shoes. "I was always quiet back then."

"You?" Robin asked.

"Yes, me." Pussy walked to a separate closet and pulled out a purse. "I was actually a shy child. My mother didn't have me interact with many people growing up."

Pussy walked up to the doorway. Robin stood up straight. "I had a lot of things going for me, but it was Coney who helped bring them out."

"She sounds pretty great," Robin said.

"She is." Pussy caught herself. "Was."

Robin took a step back as Pussy walked past her to her robe. Pussy transferred the vials from the robe to her purse. The next stop was the safe.

The bookcase hiding the safe slid easily to the side, and Pussy turned the dial until she heard a firm click. A twist of the handle completed the operation. Stacks of papers and files sat on the bottom section of the safe. It was the money stacked up on the upper shelf that was her target. She pulled out two large bundles of bills and put them into the purse. The safe closed back with a heavy sound, and she hid it once more behind the moving display of books.

"We need to head back downstairs. I want to make sure Robby is comfortable before I go."

"What about me?" Robin asked.

Pussy looked her way. There was a fragile look to her. Like a porcelain doll sitting on the edge of a shelf. "I know you're okay. I've seen you handle yourself in tough spots before. I need you to help me with your brother. Can you do that?"

"Sure." A smile cracked Robin's lips. "Thanks."

"Now, let's get downstairs." She went to the door. It barely made it past a crack before she stopped. An unfamiliar voice rose up from the floor below.

"What's going—" Pussy held up a finger, stopping Robin's words cold.

The door moved another two inches. Pussy angled herself to look downstairs. A woman and a man were talking to Robby. The woman had on a suit. The man wore a police uniform.

"Dammit." Pussy closed the door as gently as possible. "They're already here."

"Who? The cops?" Robin leaned to one side as though she could see past Pussy and the closed door.

"Yes. And I'm not willing to sit here and hope they go away."

She walked past Robin and stopped in the middle of the room. Turning in a circle, she weighed her options. None of them were good. She turned to the window.

"What are you going to do?" Robin hadn't moved.

"Nothing smart." Pussy opened the window. The pleasant spring air wafted into the room. She stuck her head out the window. The architecture of the club her second story apartment closer to a third story space. A small ledge ran along the side of the building, but that was the only structure of any sort. She craned out a little further and spotted the gutter downpipe on the back corner. A full dose of Fizz would make the jump easy, but she wanted to hold on to her limited supply. The only option made itself clear.

"Robin, I want you to stay up here." She sat down on the nearby chair and pulled off her shoes, putting them into her purse. "If for some reason the police make their way up to the room, do your best to delay them. Don't do anything to get yourself in trouble, but…well, you get the point."

"Sure thing, Pussy." Robin hurried over to the chair. "But what about you?"

"I'm just going outside for a walk. Everything will be fine." She stood up and smiled down at Robin. "And one more thing, when I go outside, I want you to close and lock that window."

"Are you sure? Shouldn't I wait to find out if you need to get back inside?"

"I won't. One way or another, I won't." She put her hand on Robin's shoulder.

Robin lurched forward and embraced Pussy in a tight hug. "Be careful."

"I will. Don't worry." The hug lingered. With great care, Pussy pried herself out of it. "You take care of yourself."

"I will." There was an odd look in Robin's eye.

Pussy wasn't sure what the young woman was thinking of doing, so she made the next move and stepped back. Starting with her left leg, Pussy exited through the window.

Rising up, Pussy kept her back against the cool brick of the wall. One step at a time, she inched along the ledge. Each footfall moved her closer to her destination. Five steps in she heard the window close, but she didn't look to make sure.

It took her a solid ten minutes to make it all the way to the corner. Her hand fell onto the heavy clay downspout and she took a look down. The street was empty. Just a couple of trashcans near the spout.

Holding onto the pipe, she turned and planted her feet and began to walk backwards down the wall. Everything was going smooth and easy. Which was her biggest concern.

The sound of the car door turned her head. Both of the cops she saw in the club were at their patrol car. And they weren't alone. A familiar face was standing there talking to the woman.

"George?" she whispered.

Hanging on the side of the building she was too vulnerable. Too visible. She couldn't wait any longer. Pussy let go of the pipe and dropped down. Both feet hit the ground without making any sound. Her purse hit the trash can.

Without looking, she ran behind the club. She dashed to the far side of the building and threw up her hand the moment she hit the sidewalk. A cab slipped over to the side of the road, and she jumped inside.

"I want you to drive around the block." She pulled a twenty from her purse and handed it over the back seat. "And take about two hours to do it, please."

The cab pulled away from the Kit Kat Klub like nothing was wrong. Pussy leaned back and considered her options.

Chapter Five

"So this is the Kit Kat Klub."

Lila shut the door of the car and pulled out a cigarette. She idly tapped it against the palm of her other hand while she looked over the front of the building.

"Yeah." Officer Stye pried himself out of the driver's seat and adjusted his pants. "Never been much for clubs, myself."

"Really? That surprises me, Stye. I've always thought of you as a real man about town." The cigarette made its way to her mouth and she snapped a match to life. Two puffs in, and one exhale out.

"Yeah, funny." He waddled over beside her. "What are you hoping to find here?"

Lila looked over at him. "I won't know until I get inside."

"Yeah, well, just to warn you, it might look fancy from the outside, but you can never trust looks. There are rumors about this place. They say it's nothing but trouble."

"Thanks. I'd hate for a cop to have to deal with trouble." She stepped away from him and started towards the door. The sound of his heavy feet hitting the ground was right behind her. "So, who says it's trouble?"

"I'd rather not say." His breathing sounded a little labored as they walked up the wide set of stairs leading to the front door. "I get the feeling it's more personal than anything else."

"The lieutenant?" Lila asked.

"I said I'd rather not say." There was a bit of gravel in his voice. She tried not to smile, but not too hard.

A poster hung just outside the entrance. A glamorous shot of a pretty young feline woman. The name underneath it read Pussy Katnip, and proclaimed that she performed nightly.

She reached for the handle. The door opened easily. "Seems inviting enough." Lila walked inside. The lush decor was the only thing that greeted her. "Yeah, this place sure does look dangerous."

"Always with the wise cracks," Stye muttered.

Lila walked down the short hallway. Standing at the top of the stairs she looked over the club. Only one person was visible, so she made her way towards him. He stood behind the bar, restocking liquor bottles.

"Excuse me," Lila raised her voice a bit and pulled out her badge. "Detective Lila Ringtail, MTPD."

The young man, an avian in his mid-twenties, all but jumped out of his socks. He juggled one of the bottles. Despite the bottle's best effort, it stayed in his hands.

"What? Geez, doll, give a guy a warning next time."

"That's Detective Doll," Lila answered. "I wanted to ask you a few questions."

She saw his eyes wander down and back up. He shook his head. "Yeah, uh, sorry about that." A cough cleared his throat. "What, uh, what can I help you with officers?"

"Let's start with something simple. What's your name?" Out of the corner of her eye, she saw Stye pull out a pad and pencil.

"Robert Thrush. My friends call me Robby, though." He leaned over the counter a bit. "I bartend here."

"Good. Just the person I want to see. You meet a lot of people here, do you, Robby?" she asked.

"Sure thing!" His face twisted up into a near comical expression. "What's this about?"

She pulled the clutch purse up and held it in plain sight. "You recognize this?"

He gave an awkward laugh. "It's a purse."

"A pretty distinctive one, too. High end. Rather glitzy, if you ask me." She pulled it back and looked at it. "Something like this tends to stand out. And being the bartender, I was hoping that you might recognize it."

"Nope." He stood up and grabbed a rag. "Sorry, not a purse guy, I guess."

"Are you sure?" She opened the purse and pulled out the book of matches. "I found this inside. It says Kit Kat Klub on the outside. Do you recognize those?"

"Yeah. Yeah, those are our matches. So what? A lot of people have them. She coulda gotten them from anyone." Robby answered.

"Who could have?" Lila retorted.

"The, uh, the lady who's purse you got. I mean, purses normally go with dames, right?" He tossed the towel onto his left shoulder.

"Sure. I'm just surprised that you went to the owner of the purse rather than the matches or the purse itself. Seems like a bit of a jump to me." Lila put the matches back in the clutch.

"Oh, well, I'm just the jumpy sort, I guess." He pulled the towel back down. "Hey, do either of you want to wet your whistle? On the house."

"Definitely!" Stye stepped forward.

"Not on duty, thanks." Lila looked at Stye. He glared back up at her. She turned her attention back to the bartender. "So, how long have you worked here, Robby?"

"What's that got to do with anything?" he snapped back.

"Just making small talk," she replied. "Is that okay?"

"Well, I got work to do." Robby pointed to the bottles behind him.

"Oh, good thing we didn't take you up on that drink, then." Lila turned and surveyed the club. Her eyes lingered on the second floor landing. "What's that up there?"

"Boss's office," he answered without hesitation. "She's not here."

Lila nodded. "When will she be back?"

"Don't know. She doesn't tell me everything."

Stye let out a heavy sigh beside her. She looked back at him. "This kid don't know a thing. Can we get outta here?"

Lila pulled an ashtray over towards her. She took one last, long drag off it and then crushed it out. "I suppose."

"What's going on?"

The voice caused all three of them to turn. A tall male canine in a formal firefighter's uniform looked back.

"George!" Robby almost ran around the bar. "What are you doing here? The club doesn't open for a couple more hours. You should leave."

"I came to see Pussy." He pointed at Lila. "Who's she? And why does she have Pussy's clutch?"

Lila smiled. Robby winced.

"I'm Detective Lila Ringtail, MTPD." She held up the purse. "You recognize this?"

"Of course I do," George stepped towards her, "it belongs to Pussy. Did she lose it?"

"Oh, that ain't Pussy's, George. Her's ain't nearly that fancy. I've never seen that thing before," Robby insisted.

"What are you talking about, Robby?" George pointed to the purse. "I'd recognize that clutch anywhere."

"You said Pussy. Do you mean Pussy Katnip?" Lila asked.

"Of course. What's this about?" George asked in reply.

"I didn't catch your name, Fireman." She extended her hand.

He took it and gave a firm shake. "George Pup. And actually, it's Chief George Pup."

"Well, it's good to meet you, Chief. Would you mind answering a few questions?" Lila gestured towards a table away from the bar.

"Not a problem." George walked towards the table.

"Stye, why don't you stay here and talk some more to Mr. Thrush. Get some of his personal information." Lila suggested.

"Why?" Stye replied.

Lila clicked her tongue. "Because it's your job, I suppose. That good enough? Or do you need me to explain that, too?"

His eyes narrowed and the mumbling returned. "Bad enough I have to take orders from someone like you."

"Sorry, didn't catch that." Lila remarked.

"I didn't say nothin.'" He grabbed his pad and tapped it with his pencil. "Just takin' notes."

She left it at that. George had already taken a seat so she walked over and took the one across from him.

"So, tell me about Pussy Katnip?" Lila began.

"I'd like to know why you want to know first, if you don't mind Detective." George's voice had a sharper edge now.

"Ms. Katnip is a suspect in a crime. I'd like to talk to her." Lila pulled out her cigarettes and lit a new one.

"Crime? What kind of crime?" he prodded.

She took a long drag and let the smoke slowly escape from her mouth. He had steel in his eyes. Lila decided to give him the answer. "Murder."

"What?" He almost choked on his reply. "You must be joking."

"I'm not."

"That's not possible. No. Pussy could never do anything like that." He shook his head the entire time he spoke.

"Why not?" Lila tapped the ashes off her cigarette.

"Because! She's…Pussy." George tapped his fingers on the table. "You'd understand if you knew her."

"I don't know her. That's why I'm talking to you," Lila said. "So, tell me why. What about her makes you so sure?"

"Look, I can't say that Pussy is a saint, but I can say that she's a good person. Everyone could tell you that." George answered.

"Good people can make mistakes, too." She took another drag. "She ran from the police, Chief."

"She must have had a good reason." George leaned back in his chair and crossed his arms.

"The officers saw her with the victim. There was blood on both of them," she explained.

George sat in silence. She could see him trying to form the words internally.

A gasp came from above, followed by the faint sound of a door clicking shut. Lila was on her feet in a second. She walked towards the stairs.

"Hey, you're not allowed up there!" Robby shouted.

"And yet, here I go." She took the steps one at a time, but in quick order. Sensing something, she glanced to see George only a couple of steps behind.

She wasted no time at the door, opening it and stepping through in one action. There was a young woman standing defiantly just inside.

"And who might you be?" Lila asked.

"You have no right to harass Pussy this way!" Robin all but stamped her foot when she spoke.

"Robin, what are you doing up here?" George asked.

"Hiding," she answered. "I saw those cops come in, and I got scared."

"There's no reason to hide," George answered. "They aren't here to do anything but talk."

"And I'd really like that option right now," Lila added. "So, let me ask this again: Who are you?"

The girl stood with her arms crossed.

"That's Robin. She's Robby's younger sister," George answered. "She works the door here most nights."

"And why were you up here when we arrived?" Lila asked.

Robin remained silent.

"Robin, you're not helping being so quiet," George said. "You should answer the detective."

"Pussy would never hurt anyone! Especially not Coney!" Robin answered.

"Who's Coney?" Lila asked.

The red of Robin's cheeks went pale pink.

"All right, why don't we all go downstairs and have a nice, big talk." Lila stepped to the side, leaving space for Robin to walk past. Then she waited for George to follow. She took up the rear.

"Stye!" she shouted from the top of the stairs. "Bring Mr. Thrush over to the table, would you?"

Reaching the table, Lila crushed out her cigarette in the ashtray and stepped back. Robin, Robby, and George sat in the chairs. Stye was several steps away.

"Okay, let's get everything out in the open." Lila began. "First off, it's pretty obvious that Miss Katnip came by here already. How long ago?"

The siblings stayed quiet.

"Hey," George began, "this is serious. The two of you might think that you're helping Pussy by not saying anything, but you're wrong. If anything, she needs to come to the police to clear this up."

"That'd be a start," Lila said. "Right now I just want to know what Miss Katnip said, and how long ago she left."

Robby looked at his sister, and then back at the detective. "Okay, yeah, Pussy came by. She told us that Coney was dead, but didn't say much else besides that."

"She said it was…." Robin's voice faded off.

"Said what?" Lila prodded.

"She said it was a dragon," Robin muttered the words under her breath.

Lila felt her eyebrows raise. "Okay. I wasn't expecting that."

"Look, I met Coney last night. She was…well, she was having a rough night. You could tell that Pussy and her were good friends, though. Pussy wouldn't do anything to hurt her." Robby's voice tried to sound confident, but didn't quite make it all the way.

"Can anyone confirm that?" Lila asked.

No one said anything.

"That's not good," Lila stated. "How about the other half of this? When did Pussy leave?"

"About a half hour ago," Robby answered.

"Yeah, that's right," Robin agreed.

"Now we're gettin' somewhere." Stye stepped closer. "Where was she heading?"

"Relax, Stye." Lila took a few more steps away. Her eyes scanned over the room. "Well, I think we're done here."

"What?" Stye almost shouted. "These kids know a lot more than they're sayin.'"

"Nothing useful." Lila looked at the gathered table. "But don't think you're off the hook. If you hear anything—and I mean anything—from Miss Katnip, you call me. Or better yet, have her call me. I'm at the Second Precinct. You got that?"

Robby looked at his sister. They both nodded.

"Have a nice day, then." Lila turned and took three steps.

"Detective," George was suddenly at her side, "I'd like to go with you. I know a lot of the regulars here, and we might be able to get them to confirm Robby's story. Plus, I have a relationship with Pussy. She trusts me. If we get the chance, well, I'd like to be there to help talk her in."

"The lieutenant ain't gonna like that, Ringtail," Stye groaned.

"Sure. I'd love to have your help, Chief," Lila said. "Just promise me that you're gonna help bring her in and not get away."

"Pussy's innocent. I know it. And the easiest way to prove that is to get her to come in and explain what happened. I just want you to give her a chance." He stuck his hand out. "Deal?"

The corner of her mouth turned up. She took his hand. "Deal."

"Aw geez," Stye mumbled. "You're making a mistake, Ringtail."

"Imagine that," Lila replied. "After you, Chief."

He led the way. Lila watched his every step. By the time they got outside Stye's grumbling had made it to open complaining.

"All right, let's get to the precinct. I've had enough of babysitting you today." Stye walked over to the driver's side of the car and climbed inside.

George looked over at Lila. "Babysitting?"

Lila shrugged. "Long story."

"I imagine," George laughed.

The sound of metal crashing came from the alley. Both of them looked that direction. One of the garbage cans was laying on its side.

"What was that?" George asked.

"Alley cat," Lila answered. "At least, that's my guess."

George stepped over and opened the front car door. "Detective."

Lila stood there for a full second. The smile that grew on her face was well beyond her control as she moved into the car and sat down. George closed the door and the made his way to the back seat.

They headed off towards the Second Precinct.

Chapter Six

The shadows seemed to stretch for blocks. It was that time of year when the days started becoming noticeable, and the nights just a short rest.

Pussy stood beside the cab in the growing twilight of the day and slipped a bill to the driver. "Wait here. Keep the engine running. I might be in a hurry."

"Yes, ma'am!" The man's enthusiasm was obviously financially driven. That worked fine for Pussy.

Keeping close to the building, Pussy made her way around the corner and towards the front door. She turned up her collar and glanced to the side. The lights were on at the Kit Kat Klub. Hiding from it turned her stomach. Not enough to make her sick, but just enough to make her hate the evening.

She stopped at the entrance to her destination. Not her club. Her competitor's.

The neon spelling out The Dogg House had a letter that kept flickering on and off. Pussy chuckled slightly every time it read The Dogg Hose.

Stepping inside, her first thought was that it must be a slow night. There were probably three dozen people in the club, but it was far from capacity. By this time The Kit Kat likely had twice that number.

Looking at the owner, however, changed her mind. He seemed happy to have that many people. A different world in the same business. She wandered her way towards him.

"Hello, Boss." Her voice was honey.

He turned quick enough to spill the drink in his hand. It sloshed out, missing her, but making a mess nonetheless. "Pussy Katnip? What are you doing here?"

It was about as warm a reception as she expected. She and Boss Dogg had butted heads far too many times to be completely civil in any situation. "Can't a girl come over for a visit?"

"Of course she can," he chewed his cigar with vigor, "but that has nothing to do with you. Or why you're here. Spill the beans."

"Can I buy a drink first?" She slipped onto a stool at the bar.

A cute young filly walked up across the bar from her and looked at Boss Dogg. He waited a moment, but then gave the bartender a small nod.

"What can I get ya?" Her voice had a distinct country twang.

"Whiskey. Make it a double. Best you've got. Neat." Pussy slid a bill onto the counter. The bartender's eyes darted from the cash to Pussy and back again. "Keep the change."

"Thanks, sister!" She grabbed the money and quickly moved to the bottles on the back wall.

"All right, now tell me why you're here." Boss Dogg stood beside the next seat over, doing his very best to loom menacingly.

"I don't want any trouble, Boss. I just came over to talk to you for a bit." The bartender returned with a glass that was well past a double. She put it down with a smile.

"Then talk. I got a club to run, and every time you come over here it ends up being bad for business." He puffed his chest out a little further. To her, he didn't seem bigger, just full of air.

Pussy picked up the glass and took a drink. The rough burn hit the back of her mouth and continued down her throat. She put it back down, reconsidering the money she just spent. "It's a little bit complicated, Boss. You sure you want to talk about it out here?"

"Yeah!" He pointed a finger at Pussy's nose. "If you're out here, you ain't gonna pull any one of your tricks. This way, I can keep my eye on you."

"Which reminds me, how is Mugsy?" she asked.

"Limping," he replied. "And you better hope he doesn't see you here. He's carrying a bit of bad blood towards you right now."

"What else is new?" she mumbled. Her voice went up. "I want to know about someone here in town. I figure you might be able to help me with that, considering the circles you run in."

"I don't know what you're talking about." He pulled the cigar from his mouth. "I'm an upstanding citizen."

"Right." Despite her better judgment, Pussy took another sip of the whiskey. "This is a special case. You might not know anything about it, anyway."

"Hey! I know everything that happens in Mutt Town! Go ahead and ask." He shoved the cigar back in the corner of his mouth.

Before Pussy could say anything he held up his hand. "Wait a second! Why should I tell you anything? What's in it for me?"

Her hand played along the edge of the whiskey glass. "How about…." She pulled her hand back and turned towards him. "What if I leave you alone for a full month? I won't come over here. Won't bother you. You'll be on your own."

"So, you won't come over here? You won't stick your nose in my business? At all, for one month?" He rubbed his thick chin, pushing aside the hanging jowls each time his hand moved.

"I…. That's right." Pussy bit her tongue. "You'll be scott free for a full month."

"I'll have no Pussy Katnip," he mused.

"Not unless you come over to my place," she answered. "But," she held up a finger of her own, "the deal is off if you can't give me any information. Usable information."

He chewed on the stogie, further mutilating the well-worn cigar. "All right. Fair enough. Ask away."

She lowered her voice, careful to keep it just loud enough to be heard over the band playing the room. "What do you know about a dragon in town?"

"What? Drago?" Boss Dogg yanked the cigar out of his mouth. "What the devil are you doing getting tangled up with Drago?"

She closed her eyes halfway and smiled. "Drago? Yeah. That's right. Tell me what you know about him."

Boss Dogg leaned in a little closer and lowered his own voice. "Look, Katnip, I know that you and I don't exactly see eye-to-eye, but you don't want any part of him. That fella works on a different level, if you catch my meaning." There was an odd sincerity to his tone.

"Just tell me what you know," Pussy insisted.

"You really don't know who Conner Drago is?" Boss Dogg asked.

Pussy said nothing, and took another sip of her drink.

"Okay, fine. Conner Drago owns the Velvet Arms Hotel. The fancy one in Big City. It lets him look like he's rich because of it." Boss Dogg chewed the cigar from one corner of his mouth to the other. "That's not it. He's got the hotel to hide the fact that he got rich from other means. Drago has got fingers that reach far away from this place. He's involved with the families around the world. That clear enough?"

"Organized crime," Pussy stated.

"You didn't hear that from me." Boss Dogg looked around the room, and then went right back to talking. "Anyway, the rumors have him involved with just about every big money job Big City's ever seen. I'm not talking penny ante stuff here, Katnip. I mean there's more money changing hands in one day with him than you and me will see in our lifetimes. So, when I tell you that you don't want to go there, listen to me for once."

"Do you have any specifics?" Pussy asked.

"I don't ask, and I don't want to. I try to stay as far away from things like that as I can."

"So, why haven't I heard of him? Why haven't the police brought him down, if he's so well known?" Pussy crossed her legs over as she turned her whole body towards Boss Dogg.

He laughed. "Yeah, well, I can't say anything about what you know, but the police…." Boss Dogg pulled the cigar from his mouth and held it in front of him. "This cigar cost me plenty of money, you know that, Katnip? It don't matter. Truth is I don't mind spending the money. Mostly because I like the way it tastes, but also because I want folks to see me with something like this."

He stopped. Pussy waited but he stayed quiet. "I don't understand."

"I spend money on cigars. Too much money. That's because these cigars aren't supposed to be sold in this country. It's illegal. But I know the right connections, and when you put the money in the right hands, things come to you." He put the cigar back in his mouth. "I think you need to remember that just about anything can be purchased."

Pussy felt her jaw tighten. "He owns the cops."

"Rents, Katnip. Just rents."

Her hand tightened around the glass. She heard the sharp sound of it fracturing and eased her grip. "So, if he wanted, he could do just about anything. Maybe even bring in someone— or something—that most people would think impossible."

"Ain't nothing impossible for someone like him. It's just more expensive."

"But why would he care about Coney?" she mumbled.

"What was that?" Boss Dogg spoke a little louder.

"Nothing. Just thinking out loud." Pussy pushed the glass away from her. A thin line of whiskey worked its way out through the crack.

"Katnip!" Pussy recognized the howl. She turned to him with a smile. He hobbled towards her with a snarl on his lip.

"Hi, Mugsy. How's your leg?"

"Is she buggin' you, Boss? You want me to take her to the door?" Mugsy pounded a fist into an open palm.

"Calm down, Mugsy. Pussy was just telling me that she was going to be out of our hair for a while. About a month, right?" There was more than a hint of obnoxious to his tone.

"Yes. That's about the sum of it." The words squeezed out through tight lips and clenched teeth.

"No kiddin'?" The smirk on Mugsy's face was asking for her to wipe it off.

"One more thing, Boss. Why the fear? Have you had a run in with Drago?" she asked.

"Drago?" Mugsy replied first. "You're going after Drago?" He started laughing. "Nice knowing you, Katnip."

"To answer your question," Boss Dogg spoke over his henchman, "no, I've never even met Drago. And I'd let you talk to everyone I know who has, but they aren't around to have conversations any more."

"Oh, I see." Pussy stood up.

"Katnip, I'm gonna tell you one more time: Let this go. Whatever it is that's got your hackles all up in a tuft, just let it go. It's better to be mad for a long time than to yell for a few seconds." She wasn't expecting his voice to be so calm.

"Thank you, John." He didn't flinch when she used his real name. "But this is something that I have to do."

"It was…well, not really good, but knowing you was interesting, anyway," he answered. "Mugsy, would you escort Miss Katnip out of the club?"

"I'd be happy to, Boss." Mugsy stood up as tall as his bum leg allowed.

"Good night, Boss." Pussy gave a slight nod.

"Good bye, Katnip." Boss Dogg turned and walked away.

She watched him walk for a moment, and then turned to find Mugsy towering over her.

"You need to take a step back, Mugsy." There was something cold in her voice, and she felt it in her heart.

"Oh yeah?" She marveled at his witty comeback.

The tension in her hand clenched into a fist. She pulled it behind her back. "This has been a bad day, Mugsy. A very bad day. I would love to have a way to let out my frustration." Her eyes narrowed to slits. "You do not want to be that outlet."

Mugsy's right hand moved down to the side of his leg. He rubbed it lightly. "You…you're lucky that there's a good crowd tonight. Otherwise—"

"Otherwise your other leg would be broken before the night was done." She walked past him. Her shoulder went into his chest, pushing him aside. Each step was a little harder than the previous as she went to the exit.

"Katnip!" Mugsy yelled. She paused. "I hope Drago rips your head off."

She chuckled. "I love you too, Mugsy."

The words didn't sink in until after she was halfway back to the cab. An eyebrow went up. "Rip my head off…."

The thought of going back briefly when through her mind, but Mugsy was already mad enough. Pushing it more would lead to a fight, and this wasn't the right time for that. She kept walking.

The cab's engine was running. The cabbie's hat was pulled down over his eyes. The movement of his mouth and chest suggested that he was snoring.

She opened the back door and sat down. He lurched. His hat flung from his head and he did his best juggling act to keep it from hitting the floor.

"Thank you for waiting," Pussy commented.

"Yeah. Yeah, glad to, uh…so, where to, lady?" He pulled his hat back on and looked at her in the rearview mirror.

"The Velvet Arms Hotel," she answered.

"That's a pretty swanky place. You sure?"

"Quite sure, thank you." Pussy smiled at him.

He put the cab into gear and drove off.

Chapter Seven

"All right then…." The file folder made a distinct thump as it hit the top of Lila's desk. The whine of her chair when she sat down was much higher in pitch, but softer in volume. "We've contacted twenty-three of the people you named."

"And?" George leaned forward and rested his arm on her desk.

"And seven of them report Pussy Katnip having a loud, verbal confrontation with a woman matching our victim's description." Lila flipped open the folder, but didn't look at the contents. "That's not a good sign for your friend."

He leaned away from her. "I still don't believe it. I know Pussy."

The folder closed back without a sound. "Look, George, I've done a little research about our Miss Katnip. It seems she has quite the reputation. There have been some stories about her that are kind of hard to believe, in fact."

George clasped his hands together. "Pussy is a unique person. Let's just leave it at that."

"Sounds like you know more than you're willing to share."

"I'm more than willing to share anything that I think is relevant. What you're talking about isn't."

Lila pulled out her cigarettes and held out the pack towards George.

"No thanks." He held up a hand to go with his words.

She shook out a butt and then tapped it twice on the desk. Her other hand flicked a match to life and brought it to the end. A long drag brought the flame into the tobacco and she held the smoke for a few seconds. Then she blew it off to the side.

"Okay, then tell me where I can find her?" she asked.

George laughed. "I can't. Not because I don't want to, either."

"You have no idea where she might be holding up?" She tapped the cigarette on the ashtray. It was too new for anything to come off.

"My first thought would be at the Kit Kat, but I'm guessing she's not there," George answered.

"Haven't heard from the crew inside the place. They would have seen her come in. Or at least any commotion that was out of place when she got there." Lila stood up and walked to the window. The streetlights cast an odd amber tint to her color.

"I figured you had someone watching the place," George said.

The rapping sound of knuckles on wood was much more pleasant than the voice that followed. "Ringtail! Lab says they won't have the report until tomorrow. And the lieutenant wants you in his office at 9:00 am sharp."

"My weekly pep talk?" she answered.

"Yeah. And he's gonna give you a cupcake, too." Stye waved as he walked off, but it was less a farewell and more a dismissal.

"He's a pleasant fellow," George commented.

"One of the pips." Lila moved to her desk and dropped the file folder in the top drawer. A twist of the key, and then she moved it to her pocket. "C'mon, it's time to get you home."

George stood up as she walked around to meet him. "I can get home by myself. Thanks, anyway."

"I'm sure you can," Lila answered, "but you're not going to. You are the only solid lead I have right now, so I'm not taking any chances with you."

"I'm a lead?" George pointed to his chest. "You're in bad shape, then."

"You have no idea." Lila grabbed his arm and gave a gentle push forward.

She walked behind him all the way to the door. Four people said good night to him. But only to him.

The fresh air hit her lungs like a gallon of water poured into a sack. She pulled out another cigarette and lit it immediately.

"This way." She started down the street. George hurried to catch up to her.

"I live the other direction." His right hand pointed back over his left shoulder. She kept walking straight ahead.

"Good to know."

"Well, isn't the plan to get me home safe?" he asked.

"Sure." She turned and smiled at him. "But my car is this way. And I figured it was probably better than walking the whole way."

"Oh. Yeah. Sorry."

"You always apologize like that?" she asked.

"Like what?" He turned to look at her.

"With that soft sound. That little embarrassed thing in your voice."

"I'm not embarrassed." His volume went up.

"Never said you were. I just said you had that sound to your voice." She took a long drag and dropped the butt on the ground, stepping on it as she passed.

"Why would I be embarrassed?"

"Beats me. I just pointed it out. Do you know why?" she countered.

"I don't even know what we're talking about!"

Lila stopped. George did the same. Both of them turned orange under the light of a flashing neon sign. The corner of her mouth went up.

"Come on." She grabbed his arm again, but this time she pulled him behind her.

"Where are we going? Why are you taking me in here?"

"Because I don't like to drink alone." The sign above the door read McSorley's Old Ale House. The place smelled like old sweat socks soaked in rum and left out in the sun for a week. She breathed it in and closed her eyes.

The far end of the bar was open, and she took George straight to the last two stools. There was barely enough light to see each other, let alone anything else.

"Lila!" A booming voice carried through the musk of the room. A massive bull of a man stepped to the other side of the counter.

"Evening, Dante." She jerked a thumb to her left. "This is George. He's with me."

"Nice to meet you." He stuck out his hand. George's was swallowed up when he shook it. "Any friend of Lila's…. What'll you have?"

"Two regulars." Lila pointed to herself and her companion. George gave her a quick stare.

"You got it!" Dante walked off to get the drinks.

"So, what do you do for fun?" Lila asked.

"I, uh, well, I don't really do much. My job keeps me pretty busy, and the rest of the time…." He trailed off.

"The rest of the time you're pursuing a little Katnip, huh?" she replied. He stared back in silence. "Don't act so surprised. You couldn't have been more obvious."

"Pussy and I are friends," he answered.

"Not all the time, I bet."

Two mugs that could serve as weapons if needed were put in front of both her and George. The brew inside it was darker than the rest of the room. A smaller glass showed up beside them.

"Thanks, Dante." She nodded at him. He nodded back.

George's eyes moved from her to him and back. "I get the feeling you come here a lot."

"I feel welcome here," she admitted.

Lila took the shot and dumped it into her mug and then waited. George eventually took the hint and did the same. She turned the tankard up. The warm umber brew poured into her mouth and down her throat with little delay.

"Wow!" George's exclamation caused her to put the mug down. "That tastes like chocolate. Almost exactly."

"Yeah, I know. Good, huh?" she chuckled.

"Amazing. I'll have to find out what's in this." He took another drink.

"Maybe I'll tell you," she muttered.

"So, what's your story?" He put the mug down and looked at her.

A myriad of options ran through her mind. She chose the truth. "I grew up in Motor City. Got my start there as a cop, too. That wasn't easy. The academy was a nightmare, but I wasn't about to give up. Eventually I made beat cop. I started figuring out a few things, worked my way up the ladder, and one day caught the attention of a sergeant on the force. Unfortunately he got a job offer out of town and left." She smiled. "When he got to his new job—Captain of the Mutt Town police force—he called me up and offered me a new position. Detective." She took another drink.

"That seems like a very short version," George commented.

"It is." She found the cigarettes in her pocket and pulled them out. It only took five seconds to have a lit one in her mouth. "The longer version isn't as nice. The best part of the story is that ever since I got the job, I've done it well. Damn well. And the Captain appreciates that. Which keeps me in a job."

"You sound proud." George leaned against the bar.

"Just of what I've done. I've had seventeen cases over the past seven months. Solved each one." She raised her glass. "Best record on the force."

She took a drink. He joined her.

"I gotta say, that's rather impressive for…." His words trailed off.

"For a 'coon?" She finished for him.

His eyes almost popped out of his head. She watched his mouth move and sputter as he tried to figure out something to say.

"Hey, it's not like I've never heard the word," Lila admitted. "I've been hearing it all my life. Been called it since I was a kid. And it sucks when someone says it to your face, but you know what's worse?" She took a deep drag on her cigarette. "When someone only calls you that behind your back."

"I…I wasn't going to say that." George's voice was weak. "I was going to say 'for a cop in Mutt Town,' but that seemed too rude. I swear I never even thought to call you…that. I'm not that type of person."

Lila took a breath. "I know you're not. I figured that out earlier."

"You did?"

The stool turned with her when she twisted to face him. Her arm stayed on the bar. "When I met you earlier today, you shook my hand. You didn't look at it. You didn't hesitate. You just shook it. And then you went one step further, and actually stuck out your hand to me. To top that off, you actually opened a door for me. For me!" She shook her head. "You don't have a problem with who I am. And I don't have one with you."

She waited for him to say something, but the silence lingered.

"Hey, I didn't mean to bring the night crashing down. Sorry I brought it up." Lila turned back to her drink.

"You shouldn't be." His voice was clear and steady. She turned her head back to him. "Look, I have no idea what life is like for you. I'm not going to pretend I do. You shouldn't have to hold it in, though."

The beer in front of her beckoned, and she answered. In no time the glass was empty. "I'm damn good at what I do, George. Damn good. But if it wasn't for Captain Saunders I'd be out on the street tomorrow. Which is where most people see raccoons, anyway. We're just scavenging pests that live off the refuse other people throw away. Maybe if everyone ignores us we'll go away."

She didn't look at him. She didn't want to.

"What happened?" he asked. "There's something you aren't telling me."

Her eyebrows went up and her head turned towards him. "Now who's the detective?" He didn't say anything, so she kept talking. "My kid brother. Barry. I was sixteen. Barely in school, but only because the school was so bad to make it almost worthless. My brother though, he was smart. Smartest kid I ever saw. And he wanted to go to the good school. Like an idiot, I encouraged him." The cigarette hung beside her mouth, supported by her right hand. "I bragged about him. My mom and dad were…those were two proud parents." The tip of the cigarette glowed in the dim light of the bar as she took a long drag. "When the cops came by the house, we were scared. Not because of anything other than the fact that they were cops. After they told us what happened to him, we weren't scared,

80

we were crying. And angry. I probably would have done something stupid, but one cop saw how I felt. He talked to me. Brought me down off the ledge."

"What happened to him? To your brother?" George's question was barely more than a whisper.

"They found him in a garbage can behind the school. The cops eventually found the scum who did it. Purists who didn't want 'our kind infecting' their school. So they made an example of Barry. But they got caught." She looked over at him finally. "And then sentenced to a whole year of community service."

He stared at her. She looked in his eyes expecting pity. When she saw anger it took her off guard.

"That's why you became a police officer. You wanted to make up for what they did."

"No. Not really. I can't make up for Barry. I'd like to think that I can be there for someone who's about to do the wrong thing, though. Make a difference in their lives. And maybe, just maybe, I can change one person's opinions about raccoons."

"I'm sure your parents are proud," he said.

She laughed. "They disowned me when I became a cop. Said that I was becoming 'one of them.'"

"Lila, I—"

"Dante!" She cut him off cold. "Bring us another round. I got some serious drinking to get in tonight."

Her eyes moved to his mug. It was still half full. "You better get that down, George, or you're going to end up with a big backlog in front of you."

She watched him eye up the glass in front of him. His hand trembled as he lifted it up and began to drink. Second by second the drink disappeared, until his glass was also empty.

Just in time to have another one put down in front of him.

"Thanks, George. You're a good man." She lifted her glass. "Bottom's up!"

Chapter Eight

"Miss Kathman!"

Pussy turned at the man's voice. As far as anyone at The Velvet Arms knew, that name belonged to her. The young man walking towards her was familiar. One of the desk clerks she spoke to when she checked in.

"I wanted to ask what you thought of your room? Is everything to your liking?"

Standard follow-up to her arrival. When you pay cash up front, they tend to cater to you a little more.

"It's lovely, thank you." She gave him a polite smile.

"Excellent. We were also able to speak with a couple of the local shop owners. One of them has offered to bring a selection of gowns here for you to look at tomorrow. I hope that will do. It was such short notice."

"Oh, of course." The hand on Pussy's purse slipped down to her thigh to rest. "Thank you for arranging it. I can't wait to see what she has to offer. It's a shame that the train people lost my baggage."

"It happens from time to time. At The Velvet Arms we strive to make everything from minor mishaps to major mistakes as painless as possible." He stood up straight and clasped his hands behind him. From Pussy's angle, it looked as though he was pushing his chest out. She held back the chuckle in her throat.

"Well, I'm going to the lounge. Just send someone to my room when the shop owner arrives tomorrow." Pussy pulled a bill from her purse and handed it to the boy. "Thank you."

He took the bill and folded it into his palm. The speed of it showed at least some practice. The boy hesitated, keeping his eyes on hers, but eventually his nerve failed him and with a nod of his head he walked away.

Returning to her original path, Pussy made her way towards The Velvet Lounge. She could already hear the piano playing. Every step made it more clear, though still quiet enough to keep the dark confines of the room calm and mellow.

Passing from the hotel proper and into the lounge was like moving from day into night. The weight of the smoke-filled air fell on her in a familiar, yet foreign way. The faint flicker of the candles lighting the room came into focus as her eyes adjusted to their ambience.

Not a particularly busy night. At least not by her standards. This was far from the familiar confines of the Kit Kat Klub. Most of the stools at the bar were empty. She made her way towards them.

"Good evening, ma'am." The bartender's voice was lush, and it matched her appearance. A jet black coat hid some of her feline features in the dark room, but accented her brilliant blue eyes. The black jacket over the white shirt only added to the look. She slid a napkin in front of Pussy with such ease that it almost seemed the napkin grew out of the bar. "Would you like something to drink this evening?"

Far from the Kit Kat Klub, indeed. "Yes, thank you. Perhaps some whiskey? Neat."

"Of course, ma'am. Is there a particular brand that you favor?" There was a hint of an accent to her voice, but Pussy couldn't place it. And the woman carried the scent of clove on her, which only added to her spice.

"Surprise me," Pussy answered. The girl nodded and took a few steps to the back side of the bar. With that time Pussy looked around the room once more. She could see seven tables with people at them. Two of those tables held only one person. She focused on them.

The first man was sitting back in his chair. His hand tapped half a beat off with the piano. A single glass rested in front of him, with a minuscule amount of ice and just under half a glass of liquid.

At the other table was a man and two stacks of paper. He was reading one slowly, and moving each sheet onto the other as he completed it. The glass on his table was empty.

"I hope you enjoy this, ma'am." Pussy turned back to the bartender. A Glencairn glass with enough liquid to hit the bulge of the tulip shape. "I find that this particular whiskey has a full nose with sugar, fruit, and light caramel notes with some treacle touches on the front side. Sweet vanilla and butterscotch follow in the rear. It all repeats in the mouth, giving a good balance and a smooth and lively flow. The finish is crisp, long, and full."

Pussy looked at the glass and then back up to the bartender. "Thank you."

The bartender waited. It became increasingly clear to Pussy that she had to taste this whiskey in front of her. She lifted the glass up and swirled the alcohol clockwise. The brown liquid clung to the glass for the briefest moment before sliding back down.

She took a sip. The warmth lingered at the back of her throat as it went down. The bartender's words began to fall into place. Particularly the vanilla taste at the end, and the crisp finish she described. "Lovely," Pussy said.

"Excellent. If you need anything else, my name is Desiree." The bartender smiled and walked away.

Pussy held back a sigh. This was a dangerous, and potentially expensive game. There was also no guarantee that it would be a success. The link between the name Drago and a dragon was flimsy enough, but flimsy was better than nothing. Perhaps that wasn't even the right word. The term desperate played around the edge of Pussy's thoughts. The glass came back to her mouth and she took a deep drink. A heady rush came with it.

The images the Fizz gave her at Coney's apartment echoed in her head. A woman smoking cigarettes. The number 837 on a box. And two dragons back to back.

Two dragons. One she met, and the other named to her earlier today. Desperation went away. Determination took its place.

The glass went into her hand as she picked herself up from the stool. A few steps later she was standing beside a table.

"Is this seat taken?" She laced her voice with as much passion as she could muster.

It took longer for the man to look at her than she expected. Nonetheless, when he did, she smiled. In different circumstances she might find him attractive. Dark eyes on a square face. Deep set canine features. There was even a hint of physique beneath the loosened collar around his neck.

"I hope I'm not interrupting." Pussy pulled the chair out, hinting like a brick.

"No." He shuffled the papers, stacking them together. His accent hinted at a Castilian origin. "I need to stop for the night anyway. I can't think of a better reason to do so."

She finished pulling the chair out and slid sideways onto it. Her hand extended across the table. "I'm Patricia Kathman."

He grasped it and turned it palm down. His lips came down, stopping just shy of actually touching flesh. "Charmed, Miss Kathman. I'm Julian Perro."

"I do hope that I am not bothering you. It's just that I was here by myself, and I noticed you sitting over here all alone, and, well, I just didn't see the point in both of us being that way."

"Not at all, Miss Kathman—"

"Patricia," she interrupted. "Or Patty. My friends call me Patty."

"Excellent. Patty it is. You are not bothering me at all. My business should have ended hours ago. I just needed a true reason to stop," he chuckled. "So, I am in your debt."

"Oh, please, I completely understand." Pussy let her fingers play along the edge of her whiskey glass. "I'm here on business myself. From The Big Apple. Yourself?"

"Unfortunately this is every day for me. I work and live here in the hotel." Julian's hand went up. Pussy turned to see a waitress heading towards the table.

"Oh really? What is it you do for the hotel?" Pussy asked.

"Actually, I don't work for the hotel. I do work here, but I don't work for them," Julian clarified.

"I didn't realize there were other businesses located here." Pussy picked up her glass and swirled the whiskey.

"It's a little confusing. I work for Conner Drago, as one of his personal assistants. Since Mr. Drago lives here, I work here. And one of the perks of the job is that Mr. Drago provides me with an apartment of my own."

"I've heard of Mr. Drago. That must be quite the experience." Pussy felt her mouth water.

"It's not all glamor. Like any job, it has its downside." The waitress stepped up to the table. "I'll have another, Karen. And for the lady another...?"

"You'll have to ask Desiree," Pussy answered. "I'm not sure what brand she gave me."

The waitress nodded and walked away.

"So, what is it you do, Patty?" Julian asked.

"I'm a buyer for a chain of fashion stores. There are a few designers here in Big City that we were wanting to speak to. We've heard good things about them. I'm here to decide whether or not to bring their designs into our locations."

"That sounds interesting. You at least get to look at new things and speak to creative people," he said.

"Yes, but, like you said, it's a job. It has its downside. I don't get much of a chance to do anything fun. It's all work, no social." Pussy stared at the glass on the table. Her thoughts were somewhere else entirely.

"How long are you in town?" Julian asked.

"Just for the next couple of days. I'm planning on checking out on Friday and going home that night," Pussy answered. She widened her eyes. "I don't suppose…. No. Never mind."

"What?" he asked.

"No, it's too pushy. Rude almost." Pussy pulled the glass up to her lips and poured some of the liquid into her mouth.

"Don't be ridiculous. What were you thinking?" he pressed.

Her lower lip went between her teeth. "I don't suppose it would be possible for me to meet Mr. Drago, would it?"

His eyes smoldered. "I think that might be possible. Mr. Drago has a small gathering of friends every Wednesday evening. He's quite the local socialite. Getting you in tomorrow night shouldn't be too hard." He winked. "I have connections."

"That would be amazing!" Pussy felt her heart race. "It's something I'll be able to tell my friends back home. An adventure of sorts."

"I'll warn you, Mr. Drago can be a little overwhelming at first, but once you get used to him he's quite the gentleman," he warned.

"Overwhelming how?" she asked.

"His intensity." His head twisted. "And his appearance. Not to frighten you, but there are not many reptilian individuals in this part of the world."

"Oh. Really?" Pussy felt her jaw clench.

"It's nothing extreme, just unusual. I figured it was better to tell you now rather than later," he said.

"Let me assure you, Julian, I appreciate you telling me that now." Pussy lifted the glass and drained it dry. Just in time for the waitress to arrive with a replacement.

"I'm glad to see that you aren't put off by it. Some people find the very idea upsetting." The glass put in front of him had a mixed cocktail. From the fruit and color, Pussy guessed it was an old fashioned.

"I like to think of myself as courageous." The new glass lost a third of its contents in a single swallow.

"I hope it's not all liquid courage," Julian commented.

She put the glass down. "No. No, that was an emotional response. I didn't mean to overreact. Sorry."

"No need to apologize, I just wanted to make sure you were okay." He took a small sip of his own drink.

"It's been a hard week." Pussy's mind flashed through the events of the day. "A hard day in fact."

"I've been there. I completely understand." His eyes wandered over her. "Is there anything I can do to help you out tonight?"

"Oh, Julian. You've already helped me. More than you realize." She kept her voice away from a growl.

"Glad to hear it."

"I can't wait to meet Mr. Drago. I don't know if I've ever wanted to meet anyone more in my life." Pussy sat back in the chair. Her body sank into the deep cushion. She couldn't recall a time she felt so uncomfortable.

Her mind was a cacophony of thoughts as the piano played in the background.

Chapter Nine

She was counting her breaths. On any other day she would just be counting out loud, but circumstances prevented it today. So to make sure that she was breathing properly, she was counting each breath.

The sky had moved from midnight blue to purple, hinting towards red. Soon enough it would shift to yellow and then blue, completing the cycle and starting a new day.

By then she would have completed her exercises, showered, eaten, and be on her way to work. At least on a normal day. Today, she was already a bit behind schedule. The thought of it made her smile.

And lose count.

Lila almost laughed as she dropped from the push-up position down to her knees. Given the options of starting over or moving on, she chose the latter. Wiping her hands off as she stood, she made her way to the window. The wiping turned to rubbing. With warmed hands, she leapt up and grabbed the installed bar above the window.

Once more the breath count resumed. Each time she dropped down she stared out over the city. Then she pulled herself up above it, until her chin and head were clear of the bar. Then the process repeated. Each time the muscles of her back and shoulders swelled.

"Uh, good morning."

"Good morning!" Lila didn't turn, but she did smile. "I'll be done here in a minute."

"Okay." George's voice was flat. It prompted her to hurry. Five more and she dropped down.

"How are you doing?" She walked to the back of the chair where she left her towel and began to dry herself off.

"I'm fine." There was something off about the way he was staring at her.

"You sure?" She threw the towel over her shoulder.

"Um," he turned his head, "you're in your underwear."

"I know," she answered. "I decided it was the best choice in case you woke up. I normally exercise naked."

"What?" He looked away from her. "But you were in front of the window."

"I know. It's okay. No other apartments have a view into my place, and the businesses across the way don't open until nine. So I'm fairly safe. No complaints so far."

"But...but there...." The sigh from him was either defeat or frustration. "I've never seen a woman exercise like that. Or...or look like you."

"I try to stay in good shape. My heritage is bad enough. Being a woman adds another level to the way people see me. I have to be ready for anything." The towel dabbed across her cheek. "Does the way I look bother you?"

"No," he replied without a second's pause. "I'm just not used to women having muscles like that."

She smiled and stepped into the kitchen. "Do you want some coffee?"

"S-sure."

She turned on the tap and moved to the cabinet. The pot and the coffee grounds came out together. The sound of the grounds hitting the metal always sounded happy to her. This morning especially so. After adding some water, she put the pot on the stove and made her way back out to the living room.

"Coffee will be ready in a few minutes," she said.

George was sitting in one of her two chairs, buttoning his shirt. "Thanks."

"You sure you're okay?" she asked.

"Uh, Lila?" His voice wavered. "I woke up in your bed."

"I know."

"I was naked."

"I know."

"W-what happened?" He finally had the courage to look at her.

"Nothing," she assured him.

"Nothing?"

"Not a thing. You were drunk. I brought you back here. You passed out in my bed. That's it."

"Then how did I get naked?" he asked.

"You took off your clothes. Right before you crawled into my bed." She heard the pot on the stove reach the boiling point.

"Oh. Okay. So…wait, you saw me?" he asked.

"Kind of hard to miss, George." She walked into the kitchen and turned down the heat on the stove.

George moved to stand in the doorway. "I'm sorry."

"Nothing to apologize for. You were a gentleman." She pulled a couple of mugs from the cupboard.

"Well, I'm still sorry that I forced you out of your own bed last night."

"You didn't." She pulled the pot off the stove and poured some of the coffee into each mug.

"What do you mean?" There was that waver in his voice again.

"I mean I slept in my bed, too. Right next to you." Steam rose up from the mug she handed to him. "Be careful, its hot."

"You slept next to me while I was naked?" He held the mug but didn't attempt to drink from it.

"That's right. It's okay, I was naked, too." She blew across the top of the coffee to cool it.

"What?" A splash of coffee hit the floor as he lost his grip on the mug for a moment.

Lila grabbed the towel from her shoulder and wiped up the small spill. By the time she stood back up, George's normally red fur was a brilliant crimson.

"George, it's okay. We slept. That's it. Nothing happened." She pushed past him into the living room. "At least not yet."

"What?" That time his voice was considerably louder.

"I've got to shower and get ready for work, George. I'd like for you to come by the precinct later today so we can go over a few things about the case." Lila took a big sip from the mug. "That okay?"

"I…I suppose so." He mumbled.

"Good." She stepped over to him and moved in close. He started to move away, but she was too quick and gave him a kiss on the cheek. "I like you, George. I want to see you again. And not just at the precinct."

"I think you've already seen all of me," he mumbled.

"You mind letting yourself out?" She was already walking into the bedroom before he could answer.

"Yeah, sure." He spoke loud enough for her to hear from the other room.

She went to the bathroom and started the shower. When she was done brushing her teeth and taking off her clothes the water was steaming.

Entering the shower her thoughts were scattered. Leaving it she was focused. Two clean suits waited in the closet. She made a mental note to talk to Mrs. Chow about having her laundry done. A glance in to the kitchen was as close as she was going to come to breakfast today. Heading to the door she paused only to pick up her keys, badge, and cigarettes. Before she reached her car she was halfway through her first smoke of the day.

Her precinct was a twenty minute drive. She used that time to review everything about the case in her head.

There were a few stares as she stepped into the building. More than the usual number. She was never this late.

"Ringtail!" Stye was the first to greet her. "You're late."

"You're gonna make detective before you know it, Stye." She walked past him headed towards her desk.

"Not to work. For your meeting with the lieutenant." Stye hurried up to walk beside her.

"Check your watch. My meeting is at 9:00. It's only 8:40." A packet waited on her desk. Before she even sat down, she picked it up. She slid her finger through the sealed flap. The familiar sound of ripping paper preceded her pulling the first few sheets.

"He moved the meeting to 8:30. He wants you in there. Now." Stye stood with his arms crossed. The sound of his foot tapping grew louder.

"Huh." She flipped through the pages. "That is a surprise."

"You know he is prone to change things like that. You were supposed to be here at 8:00. Which makes you late," Stye explained.

"Hmm?" She looked up at him. "Oh, sure. Well, I better go talk to him, then. Give him a chance to yell. I know he loves that. Let him get it out of his system. I've got work to do."

She took the packet with her, reading along the way.

"Morning Lieutenant." She put all the papers back as she walked into the office of Lieutenant C.W. Vehrka. "You wanted to see me?"

"Where have you been?" he barked.

His hair was greying, his body was more than a little past overweight, and the gravel in his voice was well worn. None of that made him appear any less intimidating.

"I started at home, and then a little later I was here. Pretty simple stuff." Lila stuck the packet under her arm and tapped out a new cigarette.

"I should have known better…." The chair under him creaked as he leaned back. "I'm taking you off the Coney Hase case."

She held the cigarette in limbo between the pack and her mouth. "I must have heard you wrong. Could you repeat what you just—"

"You're off the case. It's that simple. Gather all the material you have and I'll have Morgan come by for it in an hour." He pointed out of his office towards a detective sitting at a nearby desk.

Lila looked to Detective Morgan. He had a finger buried in his left ear. Her attention returned to the lieutenant. "Okay, sir. Just let me ask one question: What the hell?"

"Ringtail…." he grumbled.

"Lieutenant, you might not like me, and that's fine, but I have never—never—been taken off a case before. I have a perfect record and you know it." The cigarette in her hand crushed into the desk as she leaned against it. "I need you to give me a damn good reason why you're doing this."

"I don't have to give you any reason, Ringtail. I only have to tell you what to do. I just did that. Now get out of my office." His hand brushed out towards the door.

She stood still. "No."

The chair rolled back as the lieutenant pushed himself up with the edge of the desk. "What did you say?"

"As soon as you tell me why you're taking me off this case, I'll leave. Until then I'm not going anywhere," Lila put both hands back on the desk and leaned towards him.

"Do you think that I won't throw you in jail? No one will even bat an eye, Ringtail. And you would blend right in down there," he growled.

"You've been wanting to do that since I walked through the door. I just want to know what prompted you to act now. Say it and I'm gone." Her voice was echoing off the wall, just shy of a shout.

"Fine! You're off the case because I got orders to take you off it. They came down from Captain Saunders." The desk slid a little towards Lila as the lieutenant pushed off it. "There. Happy?"

She wanted to move. Her hands were still clutching the desk, preventing her from standing. One finger at a time she pulled them off. Peeling them away until she was completely free.

"Thank you, Lieutenant." She pulled down on the bottom of her jacket. "I'll have everything ready for Morgan in an hour."

"Good." The lieutenant sat back down. "Just…. I'll have another case for you before the day is out."

Pivoting on her heels she made a bee line out of his office. Her eyes landed on Morgan as she passed his desk. The notepad in front of him was covered in crude drawings of women in swimsuits.

The bile went back down her throat from sheer force of will.

Her desk chair felt cold and stiff. She shifted in it and tossed the packet down on the desktop. A few of the pages slipped out. Her head twisted to one side, squaring it with the page.

Across the top of the page it said Mutt Town Police Department. Below that was Report of Crime Scene Investigation. The words cause of death stood out halfway down. Her mind traveled down a crooked path.

"It's a witch hunt," she whispered.

"What was that?" Stye's arrival jolted her back. "I hope the lieutenant reamed you out for being so late."

"You don't know why I was in there?" she asked.

"No. Why? Was it about me? Did he say something about me?" His words came faster with each one. "I knew me tagging along with you was gonna get me in dutch!"

"It wasn't about you. What are you doing for the next hour, Stye?" Lila stood back up.

"Nothing that I know of. Why?" he asked.

"Because I have a lot of material to copy in a short amount of time." She opened her desk drawer and pulled out the file labeled 'Hase.' "I've just chosen you to be my assistant."

"What? I don't want to waste my morning helping you copy a bunch of…whatever," he whined.

She shoved every scattered page on her desk back into the envelope.

"The lieutenant told you to make sure I stayed in line, right? Well, this is the best way to make sure. You'll be right there beside me. I won't be able to get away with anything." She slapped the folder from the desk against his chest. Reflexively, his hands moved up to hold it. "Besides, I'll give you a fin if we get it done in time."

"It's gonna take forever to get this all done. I write kinda slow," he confessed.

"I'll show you the important ones. And you won't be writing. Now c'mon." Lila made her way towards the stairs. The typing room was on the second floor.

"Why you doin' this?" His feet clomped on the staircase behind her.

"The lieutenant wants me to get a copy of all my files to Morgan in an hour. I don't want to disappoint him. Not after what he just told me." She pulled out her cigarettes and shook one halfway out of the pack. It went between her lips and came all the way out.

"Who told you? Morgan or the lieutenant?" Stye asked.

Lila bit her tongue. She almost bit her tongue, anyway. "You'll make detective in no time, Stye."

"Why you gotta be like that, Ringtail?" His voice sounded a little winded.

"If I'm not, who would be?" she answered.

She opened the door to the typing room and stood to one side. The knowledge that Stye walked past her and into the room came to her, but she was concentrating on the hallway. Keeping an eye out for anyone who might be watching.

Satisfied, she went inside and closed the door behind her.

Chapter Ten

The view from her window was amazingly banal.

Pussy leaned to the right, gaining an angle to look further down the street to the left. Then repeated it the other way, so she could see down on the right.

"Nothing good ever happens here," Pussy sighed.

"Is that the truth? Or is it just what you want to be the truth?"

"Doesn't matter, does it?" Pussy answered. "One truth is as strong as any other. No matter what direction I look."

"And which truth are you wanting to see? The one on the right, or the other one?"

"Do you remember when we used to do this all the time?" The view of the street became more obscure as Pussy took a step backwards. "Look out the window and think about the future?"

"Is that what you're looking for? The future?"

"No." Pussy could see the sign for Joe's Diner lighting up the landscape. "The future is coming whether I want it or not. I'm just looking for answers."

"And you won't find them outside that window. It only holds the past. The answers are all around you."

Pussy turned towards the other voice. "In here?"

Coney shook her head. "I'm the one answer that doesn't make sense. Not if you think about it."

"Why do you say that?"

"Because, Princess." Coney turned pale. "I'm already dead, right?"

Pussy sat up like a shot. Each breath came to her in short, ragged stops. Sweat soaked sheets clung to her body like a second skin. She pushed them down and pulled up her knees. Both arms wrapped around her legs, curling her into a ball.

Her laboring airways slowed, until she was back to a normal breathing pattern. Pussy ran a hand through her hair. It felt damp and matted. The sun was already well above the horizon. A look at the clock confirmed the time.

Her legs swung out of the bed. The initial step towards the bathroom was uneasy, but only the first one.

The mirror showed her a face that looked tired and worn. The water from the tap was cold, but splashing it on her face didn't change a thing.

She turned the shower on. The hot water steamed up the room, hiding the reflection in the mirror. The feeling of it on her body washed away the sweat. The memory of the dream stayed.

Out of the shower, one towel ended up around her body and the other wrapped around her head. She wiped the steam off the mirror and smiled. It was good enough to fool almost anyone.

She made her way to the small table and chairs in her room and lifted the receiver of the phone. A second later a voice came over it.

"Velvet Arms front desk. How may I help you?"

"Good morning, this is Miss Kathman in room 518. I was hoping to order some breakfast."

"Of course ma'am. What would you like?" The woman's voice was clear and professional.

"A continental, please. With orange juice." Pussy hesitated. "Oh, and I spoke to the concierge last night. He was going to see about having someone come by with some dresses for me to look at. I'm afraid I lost my luggage. Would you ask him if he knows what time they might arrive?"

"Of course ma'am. I'll put that order in and have the concierge contact you," she answered. "Is there anything else this morning?"

"No, that's all, thank you."

Pussy hung up the phone without waiting for a reply. She went to her closet and pulled out her only dress. It felt like a day old outfit when she put it on.

She put in her earrings, then looked back down at the small dresser in the room. Her hand trembled as she lifted the necklace up. The looping silver gleamed in the morning light. All she could see was it hanging around Coney's neck. And then having it pressed into her hand.

Mindlessly, she staggered to the chair and sat down. She slipped the necklace into her clutch and stared out the window.

A few minutes later the knock came at her door.

"Room service."

She opened the door to a familiar face.

"Good morning, Miss Kathman." The concierge carried a covered tray. "I decided to kill two birds with one stone. I've brought your breakfast."

Pussy stepped back and to the side. "Please, come in."

He moved to the table and set the tray down. "I spoke with the dressmaker a short while ago. She will be here in just under an hour. At 11:00. I hope that's acceptable."

"Very." Pussy walked around to the other side of the table. "Thank you."

He lifted the cloche, revealing a plate of pastries and jam. A cup of coffee sat beside it, as well as the requested orange juice.

"That looks lovely, thank you," Pussy said.

"I've set up the Conrad room downstairs so you can view the dresses when the woman arrives." He took a step backwards. "I'll leave you to your breakfast."

"One moment," Pussy delayed him. "I was wondering…. I've heard that Conner Drago lives here. Is that true?"

"Yes, it is. Mr. Drago is one of our permanent residents," he answered.

"Where does he stay?" Pussy pulled a croissant from the tray and smeared it with jam.

"I'm not allowed to give out that information, ma'am," he answered.

She laughed. "What, do you think I'm going to break into his room and accost him?"

"Of course not. It's just policy," he laughed with her.

"Knowing his reputation, I would imagine that he lives in the penthouse, anyway." She ripped into the pastry, tearing off a healthy sized bite.

"I really can't say, but…."

A smear of jam rested on her upper lip. Pussy brought her tongue out and traced it the full width of her mouth. The concierge visibly swallowed.

"I suppose it takes something special to get up there, anyway. Some key or something," she purred.

"Something like that, yes," he mumbled.

"Well, I won't take up any more of your time." Pussy picked up the coffee cup and took a sip. The dark bitterness of the drink warmed her throat.

"Um, yes. Yes, of course." The concierge stood straighter. "I'll be downstairs when you need to…or rather when…. I'll be there at 11:00, waiting."

"I'll see you then." Pussy set the cup down. "Thank you for bringing me breakfast."

"My pleasure, Miss Kathman." He walked to the door. "Enjoy your breakfast."

As the door shut, Pussy tore the croissant in half. The rest of her breakfast continued in silence.

Ten minutes before 11:00 she headed downstairs.

The echo of her shoes reflected back down on her from the high ceilings of the lobby. The concierge desk was empty, but she walked to it anyway. A few employees nodded as they passed, but no one came over to speak to her.

"Miss Kathman!"

Pussy turned to the voice. The concierge was waving her towards him from a nearby hallway.

"I was wondering if I had misheard you about the time." As Pussy walked to him, he turned and made his way down the hall.

"Not at all. We were just finishing preparing everything." He held the door open for Pussy.

An excited woman walked briskly to Pussy. "Good morning, Miss Kathman!" She extended her hand out. Before Pussy could grasp it, the other woman grabbed Pussy's hand and shook it. "I'm Pica Holartic. Thank you for allowing me to show you some of my clothes."

She was a little older than Pussy, but not by much. Her outfit was well tailored and stylish, accenting her black and white streaked hair.

"No, thank you, Miss Holartic. I'm sure you've heard my situation." Pussy replied.

"Yes, I have. At first I thought you were just here to purchase clothes for yourself. When I found out that you were a buyer for a Big Apple client, well…."

"Really?" Pussy felt her body tense. "I was hoping to keep that a secret. I find it better if the people I'm dealing with aren't trying to put on any special facade just for me."

"Oh, I'm sorry. Should I have not mentioned that?" She looked past Pussy towards the concierge. Pussy turned to look at him as well.

"I didn't realize it was an issue. I apologize Miss Kathman." There was nothing in his voice. No tremor. No fear. "Why don't I leave you two alone. If you need me I'll be nearby."

"Thank you." She turned back to the woman. "So, Miss Holartic, let's see what you have."

"Of course!" She walked with haste to a clothing rack along the far wall. "I didn't know what season you were looking for, so I brought a sampling of several designs. I hope you don't mind."

"Actually, I would prefer to see things that I could wear today. Despite anything else you've heard, I do need outfits. My luggage isn't with me." Pussy joined her at the rack.

A bright red dress caught Pussy's eye. The fabric was light and smooth in her hand.

"That's one of my favorites." Miss Holartic pulled the dress from the rack. Broad shoulders emphasized the sharp v-neck. "I designed it for a woman of your stature, actually. It's not something I could pull off myself."

"Is that silk?" Pussy asked.

"Charmeuse, actually," the woman answered. "So airy."

"It's delightful. May I?" Pussy took the dress and held it to her body. It draped like a second skin. "Well, I'll definitely want this."

"It's not the typical evening dress, but I feel it transitions well from formal day to formal night." The excitement in her voice was palpable.

"Do you have anything a little more durable? Something that I won't worry about getting a little dirty?" Pussy held her hand up in a fist as she spoke.

"I'm not sure…." She began to work through the rack, one outfit after another. "Normally my clothes are a little more refined."

"Perhaps just a dress in a more durable fabric. I just don't want to be wearing something delicate all the time." Pussy sorted through the wardrobe along with the designer.

"Oh, I do have something…." Miss Holartic moved over to a case off to the side. A few more gowns were inside, and finally she stepped back with another dress.

It was a cream color outfit with a simple top moving to an a-line skirt. There was an obvious heft to its weight.

"The fabric isn't exactly fashionable, but my mother swore by it back in the day. It's called bengaline. Very hardy." She held the dress out for Pussy.

The surface of the dress was smooth, and had an almost silk-like appearance. The weight of it was much heavier.

"I remember this. I haven't seen anything made out of it since I was a kid." She took the dress in her hand. "I think this would be perfect."

"Wonderful!"

"Well, we have a pair of outfits for me. Now let's look at what else you have to offer." For the next half hour, Pussy saw a variety of outfits and styles. And for the most part she had no idea what the designer was talking about. She was good at making it seem like she cared, however.

Farewells were made, money exchanged, and information gathered. Despite everything else, Pussy did like the woman's skills. When this was over, she planned to visit her shop again.

The moment Pussy stepped out of the room, the concierge spotted her. He met her halfway to his station.

"I trust everything went well?" he asked.

"Quite. Thank you for setting it up." Pussy turned her head. "And I would assume you heard about my position from Julian?"

"He did mention it, yes." He sucked air through his teeth after he spoke. "I don't think it was intentional. After I saw you this morning, he stopped by my desk. He wanted to inform me that you would be sharing dinner with he and Mr. Drago this evening. I mentioned that I had met you, and one thing led to another, and he mentioned your job. Again, I'm so sorry."

"It's not a problem." Pussy's fear eased.

The concierge chuckled. "Though I guess you'll be finding out how to get up to Mr. Drago's penthouse after all."

"It does look that way."

"Oh, and what a coincidence," he pointed across the lobby, "there's Mr. Drago now."

She followed his finger across the room. The hackles on her neck rose.

His back was to her. Two men flanked him on either side, and both seemed small in comparison. He wore a white suit and hat. Judging from his position and the size of the door beyond him, she estimated him to be at least six and a half feet tall. Maybe more.

"He's a large fellow," she murmured.

"Yes, he can come across rather imposing, but once you get to know him…."

"Well, I'm hoping to get to know him tonight. Maybe we'll even be able to exchange stories." Her teeth clenched. "Who knows, it's possible we even know some of the same people."

The door opened. The private elevator left enough room for he and the two men to stand comfortably. There wasn't room for much more, however. The door closed and he was gone.

"I suppose I should get back up to my room." She looked at the concierge. "I'm going to change clothes. Can I have someone come up to my room in an hour to gather this outfit and have it cleaned?"

"Certainly. Do you need anything else?" he asked.

"No. Right now I think I've got everything that I need." Pussy took a step towards the regular elevator. "And I have a very important dinner I want to get ready for."

Chapter Eleven

She pushed the butts to one side of the ashtray, making room to squash out her current cigarette. If it wasn't for the regulation demanding that only custodial employees could empty ashtrays, she would have dumped it into the trash an hour ago. Then she wondered why she gave a damn about any regulations right now.

Mostly, she hated that it was threatening to get her desktop dirty. It was also a good distraction while she waited.

She handed the files off to Morgan at 9:45, a few minutes late, but nobody said anything. Morgan took them in hand, and then promptly filed them in his desk drawer. Lila assumed they would be there until discovered by future archeologists.

Now, all she could do was wait. For what she figured was the fiftieth time this hour, she looked at the clock. It seemed impossible that it was only a quarter past one. The last time she looked it said the same thing. And for the twentieth time that hour she considered that the clock might be malfunctioning.

"Hi, Lila." She jumped at the sound of George's voice. And then internally cursed herself for not seeing him approach. He was in full uniform, holding his cap under his left arm.

"George." There was a hope that standing up covered her jittery response.

"Sorry. Didn't mean to startle you." So much for that.

"Don't worry about it. Look, we need to go. There are some things I need to take care of and you need to go take care of them with me." She opened the top drawer of her desk and pulled out a file folder. "And here. Keep this on you. Don't look at it. Just act like it belongs to you and no one else. Got it?"

"What are you talking about?" He took the folder and started to open it immediately.

"George!" The volume of her voice was low, the but impact high. He shut the folder. "You can look at them in the car. Right now I need you to walk with me out of this building, understand?"

"Sure. I'm going to want a full explanation of what's going on, though. And there are some things that I want to talk to you about as well. Private is probably a good idea for those, too." George stepped to the side of Lila's desk, waiting patiently. Her desire to get out of the building overshadowed the brief thought about his charm.

"I'm parked just down the street." She spoke low enough for him alone to hear. "I'm in the black boiler with the banged up front fender, in case you forgot. We're going outside, turning right, and not stopping until we're inside. Once the street is rolling under us, I'll tell you what's going on."

It wasn't much of a plan, but it didn't need to be. She just needed a warm body to walk with her right now, and George was the ideal choice.

"Ringtail!" Of course, even simple plans had problems. "Where are you going?"

"Out, Stye." She pointed to the door. "I don't have any work to do right now, so I thought getting food might be something I could do. George has been kind enough to offer to buy some for me. Is that okay with you?"

"Does the lieutenant know?" he asked.

"Not on company time, Stye. He doesn't need to know." Grabbing George by the arm, she pushed on, walking past Stye and heading for the door.

"Well, don't be gone too long. We got work to do around here, y'know," Stye shouted. Lila winced. Everyone heard that. All it did was make the fire under her feet a little hotter.

The door swung open and she turned on a dime. Her pace picked up.

"What's going on, Lila? You're acting odd."

Wait until the car, George. It was a simple request. She didn't say a word.

When she slipped behind the wheel of her black beauty, she let out a held breath, much to her own surprise. George shut the door on his side just as the engine roared to life.

A quick back out of the spot, and she popped it into gear.

"Okay, now, what's going on?" George asked.

"I'm off the case," she told him. "Order came from up high. From Captain Saunders."

"Saunders? Isn't that the guy who…."

"Brought me here, yeah." She pulled out her pack of smokes. It was getting thin. One made it to her mouth, leaving four behind. "And now I'm wondering why."

"Why what?" George asked.

"Why he brought me here." Her hand fumbled for her pockets. There should have been a book of matches in one of them.

That search ended when George lit one up for her. She smiled and leaned over just enough to let him light her cigarette.

"Thanks." She exhaled a long plume of smoke.

"Why are you worried about the Captain?" He went right back to the conversation.

"Because he took me off this case. I don't think he wants it solved," she answered. "He just wants Pussy Katnip arrested."

"She's innocent!" George insisted.

"I know." Lila turned onto the highway, heading south. "She was trying to catch whoever did it."

"How do you know that?" George whispered.

"Open that folder I gave you. It's crammed with all the files about the case." She waited until he had it open. "If you look at the lab report, the cause of death is poison. The cops at the scene reported seeing both Katnip and the victim covered in blood. That same blood type was down in the alleyway. So, whatever caused the bleeding, it wasn't our victim."

"And you think that means—"

"Katnip was trying to help her. The blood was either from the killer or from Katnip, I just don't know which. Judging from the description, though, I'm betting it was your friend's blood."

George was silent long enough to cause Lila to look at him. He was staring into the files, but it didn't look like he was reading them.

"What?" Lila asked.

"You're probably right," George muttered. "I…I'm not at liberty to discuss everything, but Pussy has a tendency to get herself mixed up in other people's problems. It wouldn't be the first time she got hurt in the process."

"And your just telling me this now because…?"

"It's complicated." He looked up at her. "And I didn't trust you before."

She didn't even try to hide the smile. "Why, George. If I didn't know any better, I'd say that—"

The police siren wailed to life behind them. Close behind. Lila looked in the mirror to see a patrol car right on her tail.

"That's not good," she voiced out loud.

"What do they want?" George looked back towards the encroaching car.

"If I had to make a guess, I'd say they want me to pull over." On her right Lila spotted a crane just visible above the tree line. She hit the gas.

"What are you doing?" George's voice had a little twang to it suddenly.

"Trying to get away." She glanced in the mirror again. The cop car was gaining already.

"Why?"

"George, when someone doesn't want a case solved, and one of the best detectives on the force was working on that case, what would you do?" she asked.

There was a two count before he spoke. "Rub out that detective."

"You win the kewpie, George!" She cut the wheel hard to the right, angling down a dirt road leading off the highway.

"Can you outrun them?" he asked.

"Not a chance. That's a brand new cruiser. I love this beast, but she's old." A cloud of dust was kicking up behind them, partially obscuring the pursuing vehicle.

"Then what are you going to do?"

The rough road had the car shaking like a jackhammer working granite. "I'm from Motor City, remember? We learn to drive before we can walk."

The car lurched forward, accompanied by a loud crashing sound.

"Sounds like they want to play," Lila growled. "Good. I do, too."

"Did they just ram us?" George shouted.

"And they're going to do it again." The road crested a small hill. The sight of the quarry made Lila smile. It turned to a sneer as the cruiser slammed into her car again.

"What are you planning?" George was staring out the back window again.

"A little dirt track racing." She cut the wheel hard to the left. George slammed against the passenger door. The back of the car slid out on the soft soil, leaving their vehicle angled with the road running beside the excavation.

The cops fell behind as they made the turn. She slowed down to let them catch up.

"George, you might want to hold on to something." She dropped the car down into the lowest gear. "This will be a little tricky."

She heard him mutter something, but it was too soft to hear over the sound of the engine mixed with the dirt road. Time was a precious commodity now. Taking a moment to repeat a sentence was something of a luxury.

Piles of stone in various sizes formed a crude maze to her right. On the left was the excavation pit, and a drop of unknown height.

The car lurched forward from the impact. The cruiser was firmly against the rear bumper and doing its best to force them to the left. To push them over the cliff.

She hit the brake, slowing but not stopping. The police car continued its assault, inching them over towards the pit.

"They're going to push us over the side!" George shouted.

"That's what they want to do, yeah." The words were somewhat obscured through her clenched teeth.

"What are you going to do? You've got a plan, right?" The effort George was putting into not panicking was both charming and annoying. She'd figure out which was stronger later.

"The plan is for them to try to push us off the side of this road." Lila moved her right hand off the wheel long enough to flex it. She moved it right back. "Just to not let them succeed."

This time she slammed the brakes. A whine rose from the tires as they fought against the dirt road. The dirt cloud moved from behind Lila's car to being behind the cop car. It's tires spun as it continued to force them forward.

"Lila?"

She didn't answer. He probably didn't want her to, anyway. They were only a few feet from the edge of the cliff.

"Lila!"He gripped onto the dashboard, turning his knuckles white.

It was now or never. Lila turned the wheel sharp to the right and floored it. The back side of the car twisted around as the cruiser lurched forward at a frightening pace.

Lila's car spun around completely. She looked to her right. The officers in the car threw their hands in front of their faces as the cruiser went past the point of no return.

That's when she felt their rear bumpers interlock.

Her car went backwards, pulled by the tonnage of the vehicle now plummeting down to the bottom of the quarry. They were about to follow. She wasn't going to go easily.

Turning into the angle of the pull, Lila hit the gas one last time. The car sped along the edge of the pit. Above the fall, and not plummeting down.

They might have been safe if it wasn't for the boulder.

The impact flipped the heavy vehicle to the side. Thankfully, it was away from the pit. It was still enough to send the car over one full turn and then again onto its side.

Lila would like to think that she didn't scream when it happened. Inside she knew the truth.

The world was a jumble. Something warm was on her face. The front bench seat was rising above her like an upholstered wall. Something was missing, though.

George. He was supposed to be in the front seat with her. He wasn't.

Something was growing louder. A whine. Or a scream. Or…or a siren.

Turning her head proved to be more challenging than she would have thought. The arrival of the flashing lights confirmed her fear.

"Great. They sent two cars." Her hands moved underneath her, and she pressed up.

The intent was to help her stand. But the sudden rush of blood had a different effect. Her arms buckled beneath her and her head slammed back into the broken window below.

Like a butterfly's wings, her eyelids fluttered fast enough to attempt flight. As the world faded away, she saw the uniform of a police officer approaching the car.

Her last conscious action was an attempted growl. It came out like a whimper.

Chapter Twelve

"Miss Kathman."

"Oh, please, Julian, call me Patty." Pussy spotted him the moment she stepped off of the elevator. Even if they had never met before, her eyes would have gone directly to him. His outfit looked like it cost a million bucks. And he made it look even more expensive.

"You look stunning, Patty." He took hold of her hand and extended it to a full arm's length to casually look at her outfit.

"I was lucky. The client I saw this morning had excellent taste." It was an honest statement.

"The dress can only do so much. It takes someone to wear it." He let go of her hand.

She felt her cheek flush. "I…don't think we want to keep your boss waiting."

"True," he agreed, "but it is difficult to want to share you right now. Still…."

He held out his arm. She wrapped hers around it. Together they walked towards the private elevator.

"What floor does Mr. Drago live on?" she asked.

"The eighteenth floor penthouse." He looked at her. "So, you were right about that, too."

"It just made sense. Someone of his stature would want to have an equally impressive home."

They stopped in front of the door and Julian pressed the call button.

"And it is. You'll see for yourself soon enough." The door opened. He gestured inside. "After you."

The confines of the elevator were tight. There was enough room for four, perhaps five. Or three large people. The image of Drago and his men filling it up came back to her.

Julian inserted a key into the panel and gave it a turn. Three buttons above it lit up. He pressed the top one.

"Three buttons?" she asked.

"Yes. It stops here on the lobby floor, of course. And then on the eighteenth floor and Mr. Drago's residence. It also can stop on the seventeenth floor. That's where many of Mr. Drago's employees live."

"Including yourself?" She smiled at him.

"Yes, that's right." His voice suddenly picked up a more lush tone. "It's a rather nice suite. I'd love to show it to you."

"Perhaps later," Pussy answered. "Right now, I'm looking forward to my dinner with Mr. Drago."

The elevator let out a gentle chime, and a second later the door slid open.

It emptied directly into the foyer of the penthouse. Twelve foot ceilings arched up to fifteen feet at their crest. A mural of open blue sky did its best to give the illusion of an even higher space. On either side of the door stood an eight foot tall statue of a highly stylized alligator woman holding a sword. The yellow sheen attempted to fool people into thinking they were made of gold. Attempted.

"Impressive," Pussy stated.

"Not yet. This is the entrance." Julian stepped past her. "The real show has yet to begin."

A few steps later the ceiling all but disappeared. Pussy found herself having to look up to actually see it twenty feet above her. The walls of the room looked to be crafted from limestone. A second glimpse showed it to be a faux painting technique over plaster.

Two bright red couches measuring at least ten feet long each sat across from each other. A narrow white marble table rested between them. In one corner, a curved bar was set up. A familiar looking woman stood behind it patiently. A large hallway led out the far side, and a twin doors opened out onto a balcony of some sort over near the bar.

All in all, Pussy found the overall effect amazingly tacky.

The only truly impressive sight was the wall of windows that looked out over Big City. The lights of the skyline at night were impressive enough from street level. At this height they became almost magical.

"That is impressive." She could at least sound genuine about the view.

"Mr. Drago likes to be unique." Julian looked around. "And I'm surprised he's not here. I'll go let him know that we've arrived. Feel free to get yourself something to drink."

"I might just do that." Pussy walked away from him and towards the bar. She got there just as Julian disappeared down the hallway.

"Good evening, Desiree. How are you?" Pussy smiled across the bar.

The woman looked past her and towards the hall. "What can I get you tonight, Miss?"

"I don't suppose you have that same whiskey you gave me last night?"

Desiree pulled a glass up and turned to pick up a bottle from behind her. "No, I'm sorry. I do have something comparable, however. Not quite as complex in my opinion, but it still has a full body and pleasant nose."

"That sounds fine." Pussy watched her pour the glass half full. With a twist of the bottle, Desiree pulled it back.

"Thank you." Pussy reached for the glass. She tried to yank her hand away the moment Desiree grabbed her by the wrist. She met the other woman's eyes. Something glistened across their blue surface.

"Run." Desiree whispered. "Do it while you still can. Run."

Pussy stood and blinked. "What? What are you talking about?"

Just as suddenly, Desiree let go of her. "I hope you enjoy your drink, Miss. If there is anything else that I can do for you, simply ask."

"Good evening." A voice like sandpaper over glass called her away from the bartender. Her earlier estimate was perhaps a little low. He stood almost seven feet tall. The narrow width of his shoulders made him seem even taller in some ways. His dark green skin contrasted sharply against the perfect white suit he wore. And he was smiling. A long row of sharp teeth stretching the width of his face. "I'm sorry to have kept you waiting."

Pussy felt her jaw clench tight. She forced it to relax enough to reply. "Don't think twice about it. I'm just happy that you were kind enough to invite me up to dinner tonight."

"It's my pleasure. Julian has said such wonderful things about you." He stood directly in front of her and held out his hand.

"He's exaggerating, I'm sure." She took his hand and applied a little pressure. "Besides, we just met yesterday."

"Julian can be very insightful." He waved at Desiree. She began to craft a beverage. "But please, tell me about yourself."

"Not much to say. Just a woman in town for a couple of days of work." Pussy stepped away from the bar. Drago moved in and took the drink from Desiree.

"There has to be more to it than that. He told me that you were a buyer for a firm in The Big Apple. I'd love to know who." He took a sip of what appeared to be a martini.

"And I'd love to tell you, but really I can't. Confidential, I'm afraid." Pussy took a sip of her own drink. Desiree was correct. Not quite what she had last night, but still a smooth glass of whiskey.

"That's a shame, but I understand." He stepped back, revealing the men behind him. "Oh, I'm sorry, I'm being rude. Allow me to introduce my associates."

He pointed towards the man on her left. The dark color of his fur faded away as it traveled up his neck to his weasel like face. Exposed flesh was only broken by a pair of bushy eyebrows above his beady peepers. The skin looked raw and leathery. He wore a grey suit with a similar cut to Drago's, without being as refined. "This is Tayra."

Drago moved to the man on the right. Blanche white fur matched his suit perfectly. What drew her eye was the constant twitching of his extraordinary long tail. It was hard to see from this angle, but she swore his tail split in two at the tip. The slight angle to his cat shaped eyes hinted at an eastern origin. "This is Neko Mata. He's fairly new around here."

There was only one person left. "And of course you already know Julian."

"It's nice to meet all of you." She scanned the rest of the room. "Julian told me you typically had a gathering of friends on Wednesday. Are we expecting others?"

"Not tonight. I had to schedule a social event later in the week. A special occasion." Drago took another sip. "It's just us for the evening."

"Oh, I do hope I'm not putting you out." Pussy studied the room. The doors and windows in particular.

"Speaking of out," Drago moved forward and she gave him a wide berth, "dinner will be on the patio. It has the best view in town." He opened the double doors leading outside. "After you."

The view of the city from the windows was amazing. Looking out from the balcony towards the lake was stunning. The lights shined along the shoreline. Further out all Pussy could see was darkness embracing a starlit sky.

"Beautiful," she admitted.

"Isn't it?" Drago's voice came from right behind her. "Sometimes I like to come up here by myself and just stare out into the night."

Her left hand moved to her purse and slipped inside. The passive sound of the night hid the sound of her fumbling with the contents.

A plethora of furniture decorated the balcony. The most prominent piece was the fifteen foot long table in the middle of the space. Six chairs were set up on either side. Larger, more ornate chairs capped either end. Three dinner settings awaited them.

"Only three? There are five of us." Pussy slipped the item she retrieved into the cuff of her sleeve.

"Neko and Tayra aren't eating. They are just here as employees." Drago walked over to the edge of the balcony and looked over the side. Pussy walked next to him. "It's roughly one hundred and eighty feet down. It looks like so much more."

Pussy only glanced down. A few decorative outcroppings obscured the view. Mostly all she saw were well lit trees. She returned to looking out over the sea-like lake.

"You must feel…untouchable up here." Both hands gripped the railing like iron.

"It's just a view," Drago replied, "what matters is what you see from here."

"And what is it that you see?" Pussy turned to look at him.

He turned away from her. "I see that it's time for dinner. Come. Let's have a seat."

Drago moved to the head of the table. Julian moved to his right and pulled out the chair, gesturing for Pussy to sit down.

"Thank you." She smoothed out her skirt and crossed her legs at the ankles as she sat.

"I must apologize," Drago commented as Julian took his seat, "I didn't check to see if there was any food you found unpalatable."

"It's all right. I would have shown up anyway," Pussy answered.

Three well dressed men came out with platters covered by silver cloche. Each of them stepped to the side of the respective diners and put the plate into place. As one they pulled up the cloche and stepped away.

In the center of Pussy's plate was a rabbit's foot. The end of it was still wet with blood.

Her lip pulled back and her eyes turned to fire as she looked at Drago.

"Now," Drago growled at her, "perhaps we can have a genuine conversation, Miss Katnip."

She pushed back on her chair. It only slid a few inches before running into the two men standing behind her. Tayra and Neko were just on the outskirts of her peripheral vision.

"Why Coney?" Pussy snarled. "That's all I want to know."

"Miss Hase stole from me." Drago leaned back. "And I want you to tell me where she hid my property."

Pussy put her hand on the dinner knife in front of her. "Even if I knew, there is no way that I would tell you."

"I have it on good authority that you were the last person she spoke with. And that she thought of you as her closest friend."

"I spoke with her the night before she died. She didn't say a thing. And that morning she couldn't speak a word. You had already killed Coney when I got to her apartment." Pussy shifted in the chair, leaning in towards Drago. "Or don't you remember meeting me there?"

"Miss Katnip," Drago answered, "prior to tonight, I've never seen you before in my life."

"Liar!"

"I have no reason to lie to you." He looked past her. "Mr. Mata, on the other hand, remembers you well."

The sound got to her before Pussy looked over her shoulder. The man introduced to her as Neko Mata was changing. An unnatural glow surrounded him, and his fur began to fade away. Bright white leathery skin grew onto his belly. Along his back, arms, and legs scales sprouted to lay over his flesh like armor. The long tail grew thicker, and then black spines grew out from the tip. They continued up along its length and then proceeded up his back, springing out in order until they reached his neck and head. At once, the man's hair formed into long spines and his face grew into a protracted dragon-like snout.

"What in the world!" Pussy jumped up in her chair and then back onto the table. She looked at Drago and then back at the dragon monster she had previously met. "All right, I admit, that took me off guard."

"Tell us where Coney hid my property, and you'll walk out of here," Drago commented. "Otherwise…."

"You made one mistake, Drago." Pussy slipped the vial hidden up her sleeve down into her hand. "You killed one of my friends."

She heard the roar of the beast as she downed the contents of the vial. The Fizz rushed into her body, pushing her reality to the side.

The water of the lake came into view. A ship—or perhaps a boat, the size changed constantly—docked beside a pillow-top bed. At the foot of the bed stood a figure in shadow. She reached down and plucked the boat from the water and held it in her hands. The lights from the boat illuminated Coney's face as she stared down at it.

And then Pussy found it difficult to breathe. The visions faded away, and she felt her feet dangling beneath her. A single massive, clawed hand wrapped around her throat. The wind whipped up and around her body. A glance down confirmed that she was dangling over the side of the building.

"Now, Miss Katnip," Drago stood beside his dragon henchman, "you have one more chance to tell me what I want to know."

"Funny, I was thinking the same thing about you." She shifted in his grasp. "You're going to pay for killing Coney."

"Kill her?" There was genuine surprise in Drago's voice. "Miss Katnip, I very much wanted her alive. We did nothing to Coney Hase."

"What?" She froze.

"Let's not make this messy," Drago said. "Tell me what I want to know."

Pussy brought both hands up to grab the arm leading to the claw around her throat. "No, let's do make it messy." She pulled her hands back and then slapped them together in a flash.

There was the faint sound of cracking bone that went along with the dragon's scream.

And then Pussy was falling.

She looked down. At one hundred and eighty feet up, it would only take four seconds to hit the ground. Five if she was lucky. Thanks to the Fizz, every one of those seconds seemed like ten. And she had no intention of making it to the ground.

The first outcropping was little more than a narrow ledge. She reached out for it. It slipped by just past her fingers.

The second was more prominent. A larger ledge holding decorative sculptures resembling gargoyles spaced evenly along it. And one of those gargoyles was directly below her.

Pussy had time to blurt out one thing right before she impacted. "This is going to hurt."

Her hands grappled the neck of the statue. The momentum of her fall threw her body into the solid brick wall. She heard the stone of the statue crack and felt it shift in her arms. Dropping down another two feet, she let go of the statue and grabbed ahold of the ledge. A piece of the statue fell. It bounced off her leg and plummeted towards the ground.

"I was right," Pussy mumbled, "that hurt."

She looked up. Drago stared down at her. Beside him the dragon—Neko Mata—roared. And held his damaged arm with his good hand.

The windows were too far above to reach. Below her, she could feel the top of one with her feet. There wasn't time to think about it.

Pussy pushed off with her feet, swinging up until she was almost perpendicular to the wall. And then she arced down, letting go of the ledge and allowing the force of the action to carry her both to, and then through the window.

Glass shattered around her. A shard of it ripped into her leg as she passed. To help cushion the landing, Pussy curled into a ball and rolled into the room, impacting against the nearby bed.

A look around told her the room was empty, and she thanked her luck for once. Standing made her curse it again. The gash from the broken window was deep.

"And I liked this dress." Using another piece of glass, she cut a long strip of cloth, and quickly tied it around the wound.

Blood ran down her leg with every step. And she knew it was only a matter of time before it left a trail of red behind her.

The stairs weren't far away, and they were a much safer bet than the elevator. The sign beside the door told her she was on the twelfth floor. Farther down than she thought. Still seven floors above her room, and then another five to the exit and safety.

Five floors down she was limping. By the time she got to her room, the bloody trail was clear behind her. The key to her room was in her purse along with Coney's necklace, and her purse was still on the balcony. She made a silent vow to get them back as she used her shoulder to open the lock.

A few splinters of wood littered the floor and she hobbled over them to the dresser. The remaining vials of Fizz and a roll of cash were there and waiting. She grabbed them and went back to descend the stairs.

The door to the lobby opened out to a gathering of people. From the look of things, a wedding party returning from the reception.

She didn't hesitate. Even when the gasps came at her expense. The only thing that gave her any pause was the sight of Tayra beside the front door of the hotel. But it was only a pause.

With her leg still hindering her steps, Pussy walked towards him. The weasel faced man stood up and blocked her way. "Not today, pussy cat."

Pussy's left hand reached up to grab him around the neck and pull down, while her right hand swung up with considerable force.

His head snapped back and the rest of his body followed. He hit the ground in a heap far enough away to clear her exit.

A commotion grew behind her. She ignored it and walked straight to the nearest cab.

"Where to?" the driver asked as she slipped into the back seat.

"Drive." She pushed a pair of bills his way. "Just drive. I'll figure out where in a minute."

He looked at the money and popped his hack into gear. She leaned back and let the pain fade away as the Fizz did its work.

Chapter Thirteen

She knew she wasn't dead. There was way too much pain for her to be dead. No, this was something far worse.

"Hey." His voice was soft, but familiar.

Lila did her best to sit up, and almost immediately regretted it. Her hand came up to the side of her head in a desperate attempt to grab hold of her brand new headache. She felt cushions beneath her and something to one side. Her bed was a couch.

"Where am I?" she mumbled.

"My place." George answered. "I thought it was best to bring you back here."

"Okay." Two fingers moved just enough for her to be able to fix one eye on him. "Then all you have to tell me is how I got here."

"I brought you here." He picked up a glass from the nearby table. She was pretty sure it had water in it, though she wouldn't be upset to discover gin. "Drink this."

It didn't take any more encouragement. About a third of the glass went down her throat in a couple of seconds. The back of her hand wiped across her mouth. "Great, but how? Last I remember you were nowhere to be seen, and there was a cop car pulling up. Which means something else happened. Or you can do magic. Is it the magic thing?"

"No," he answered.

"Figured as much." The clothes she wore didn't match the suit she put on this morning. "And there is still some explaining in order."

"I had some help," he said.

"Did I hear her—" The owner of the new voice stepped in from the back of the apartment. "Oh, hey Ringtail. Welcome back."

"Stye?" Lila blinked a couple of times. Finally settling her eyes back onto George. "What is Stye doing here?"

"Hey! I'm right here!" The portly man walked to the far side of the coffee table.

"Okay, then you tell me." She scanned the room.

"Well, Chief Pup here convinced me to help get you back here. When I pulled up I found him about twenty yards from your bucket. He said you was in it still, so we got you out," Stye answered.

Her hands tapped her pockets. "Now I've got the play by play, but I'm more interested in why, I suppose. You're a cop. Why didn't you finish me off?"

"Chief here said you had some crazy things going on. I gotta say, though, that question tops it all off. You're a cop, Ringtail. I got your back." He put his hands on his hips.

"Yeah, but there were a couple other cops, too. I kinda…. They're not doing too well, Stye." She turned around to look at the rest of the room behind her.

"They're busted up, sure, and they ain't got their cruiser no more, but they're alive. I saw 'em pulling themselves outta the water before we left," Stye explained.

"There was water in the pit?" She tapped her pockets again, just to make sure.

"You knew there was water down there," George stated. "Right?"

"Sure. Let's say that." Her feet slid around and she moved to a more upright sitting position. "Didn't the lieutenant send you out after me, Stye?"

"Nope. When you passed me in the precinct, I knew somethin' was up, so I followed you. If you weren't gonna tell me what was wrong, I was gonna have to find out for myself. Didn't figure it was gonna turn out that there were gonna be other cops chasin' after you, though."

Lila looked up at him. "Y'know, Stye, you might just make detective yet." She stripped every scrap of sarcasm away from the sentence.

"Yeah, well, you gonna explain what's going on to me? Chief had some wild story he was sayin', but I figure you'll have the details." Stye grabbed a chair and turned it around so he could sit across from her.

"Sure. Just one thing first." She tried not to growl. "Have either of you got a damned cigarette?"

"I smoke a pipe," George answered. "Sorry."

Stye stood back up and reached in a front pocket. His hand returned with something resembling a wash rag that was rung too hard and left out to dry. "Here."

Lila caught the object. It was a pack of cigarettes. Or at least it had been at one time. The actual pack was all but gone, but she pried it open to see a broken stub of a gasper with some lint on it.

She pulled it out and stuck it in her mouth. "Got a light?"

The sound of a striking match was followed by George bringing it in front of her. She looked in his eyes. Then Lila took hold of George's hand and pulled the match towards her as she leaned in. She dragged the fire in, and blew the smoke out.

"Thanks," she whispered.

"So?" Stye asked.

"Hmm?" Lila looked back to him. "Oh, yeah. George told you the basics. Believe him on it. The thing is, there is something rotten in the corps, Stye. I don't know who stinks, but there's more than just one, I'm sure." She pointed a finger at him. "And you and I get to find out who and why."

"Are you talking about at the precinct?" he asked.

"I'm talking about on the whole force." She sucked in more of the stale smoke. "It goes up, we just gotta trace the path. Find out how high."

"You don't mean you're going back to the precinct, do you?" George's eyes were saucers.

"Sure do. I'm not going to be able to find the answers out here. Besides, that's likely where I'm safest," Lila said.

"How do you figure that?" Stye asked.

"The fact that you aren't on the take means it's not everywhere. Just key spots. Probably the lieutenant, but—"

"Not the lieutenant!" Stye blurted out.

She hesitated. "Probably the lieutenant, but we're gonna have to check everyone. It's not going to be easy to get up the ladder. And they aren't gonna try anything against me so out in the open."

"That's not exactly the most sound reasoning I've heard," George said. "You did get hit on the head pretty hard."

"I didn't say I wanted to go there tonight." She looked out the window. "What time is it, anyway?"

"About 10:30. You've been out for a while." The phone rang. George stood up and walked across the room towards it. "And sorry about the clothes. Yours were pretty torn up."

He picked up the phone with his back to her.

"What? Where are you?" There was a new level of excitement in George's voice. Then the volume went down.

"You really think the lieutenant is involved?" Stye asked.

Her eyes were on George as she answered. "Can't say for certain. I haven't talked to him about it, but yeah." She glanced at Stye. "I do think there's a good chance."

"I can't believe it." The heartbreak in his voice was unmistakable.

"Lila?" George called her attention back. "It's for you."

He held out the receiver. Lila discovered all manner of new aches and pains as she stood from the couch. The walk over to the phone was another adventure in discomfort.

Without another word she took the receiver and held it to her ear.

"Hello?" she said.

"Good evening, Detective." The voice on the other end sounded like butter rolled in cracked pepper.

"Miss Katnip." Lila kept her voice level. "How nice to hear from you."

"I'm afraid you do have me at a bit of a disadvantage. I never did get your name," Pussy stated.

"Ringtail. Detective Lila Ringtail." She pinched the cigarette off and set it down beside the phone. "I'd be happy to give you the full introduction in person."

"Not just yet," she answered. "There are still a few things that I need to take care of."

"I'm not planning on arresting you, Miss Katnip. I know you didn't have anything to do with Miss Hase's death."

"I'm not sure that's entirely accurate, Detective." That statement pushed up one of Lila's eyebrows. "I didn't kill her, but I'm starting to think that there is something more to her death. And that I'm somehow involved."

"And just how do you figure that?" Lila asked.

"Coney came to me the other night. There was a reason for it. I just have to figure out what and why." The voice on the other end of the phone was cold.

"All right, then. So, why did you want to talk to me?" Lila picked up the cigarette again and rolled it between two fingers.

"Because I need your help," Pussy replied. "Are you familiar with the name Conner Drago?"

"Rich guy in Big City. Makes sure his name is in the social column regularly. Owns a pretty fancy hotel. That Conner Drago?"

"That would be him, yes. I also think he's connected with Coney's death."

Lila shifted in place, and move the phone to her other ear. "That's a pretty tall order. Why would someone like him be interested in her?"

"And now we've come to what I need help with," Pussy stated. "Can you look into that? Find out what Coney has been doing for the past few years?"

"You're thinking there's something specific there." Lila put the cigarette back in her mouth, but didn't light it. "Care to share what it is?"

"I don't have specifics, Detective. I'll let you know when I do."

"Assuming I agree," Lila finally answered, "how would I get ahold of you again?"

"I'll call George. Can you keep in touch with him?" Pussy asked.

Lila looked over at the fire chief. "Oh, I'm pretty sure I can stay near George, sure."

"Okay…." Pussy's voice trailed off. "Oh, can you also check into another man. Goes by the name of Neko Mata. I think he may be foreign."

"Who's that?"

"One of Drago's henchman. I spotted him at the sight of the murder," Pussy explained.

"You think he's the one who poisoned her?" Lila asked.

"Poisoned? What do you mean?" There was a sudden urgency to Pussy's voice.

"We got the tests back. Our victim was poisoned," Lila stated.

There was a faint murmur on the other end of the phone line, but Lila couldn't make out any details.

"Miss Katnip?" She made an attempt at getting her attention.

"I'm here," Pussy answered. "Did you happen to notice the overturned furniture?"

"Sure. I figured that happened in the fight," Lila answered.

"What fight?"

"The one that you had while you were there. I'm guessing it was probably with this Mata character."

Lila waited through the seconds of silence.

"You're good, Detective."

"That's what they tell me," Lila said.

"I didn't touch the furniture. It was like that when I got there. Coney...the victim's body was already on the floor. Mata was standing over her, looking straight at me when I entered. I had assumed she was in a struggle with him, but now...."

"Now you're wondering if the furniture wasn't already overturned when he got there." Lila finished her thought.

"Someone was looking for something. I think I know what. Or at least the owner of the item. Can you do a once-over on the place?" Pussy asked.

"Sure. I don't have anything better to do," Lila replied.

"Sorry, Detective, but I don't think I'm welcome there right now." Pussy's voice dripped with attitude.

"You're not welcome anywhere. Watch your back, Miss Katnip. Some police might be out to do you in."

"Thanks for the warning," Pussy answered. "You might want to watch out, too. Drago has worked his way into the force, as I hear it."

"Really?" Lila's voice went up. "Now that is information I can do something with."

"My pleasure," Pussy answered. "Can you put George back on the line?"

"Are we done?" Lila asked.

"Unless you have something else, yes. Don't worry, you'll be hearing from me."

"Until then, Miss Katnip." Lila moved the phone away from her ear. She heard Pussy mutter some sort of farewell, but not the specifics. "George. She wants to talk to you again."

Before he touched the phone, George looked her in the eye. Lila fought the urge to wink at him. Instead she just smiled and stepped away.

"Stye." The officer jumped at his name. "Give me your notebook and pencil."

"Was that the Katnip broad?" He handed her the requested items. She opened them and started to write.

"It was." She tore the sheet and handed it to him. "I need you to go to the precinct and look into these two names. Find out what you can."

He looked at the paper and then back up. "Drago? The rich guy? Why would we have anything about him?"

"Do what you can. Don't call Big City about it. Sounds like that might stir up a different hive of bees." She thought for a second. "And find out where Coney Hase was before she came to town. Check the train stations and airports. Find out if they had her as a passenger and where it came from."

"I thought we was gonna check on the lieutenant and everyone. See who was a bad cop or not." Stye folded the paper and stuck it in his front pocket.

"We are." Lila put her hand on his shoulder. "And as tough as this is to say…thanks, Stye. I owe you."

"Don't go getting all soft on me." Stye rolled his shoulder back, and she let go of it. "I'm just doin' my job."

"Right." She looked around for any matches. An open book lay on the table beside the couch.

"Sorry about that." George walked up as she lit what was left of the cigarette.

"What did she say?" Lila asked.

"Uh, nothing." George scratched the back of his head. "She just wanted to make sure I was okay."

"Got ya." She blew out less smoke than he just did. "Well, it's kinda late tonight, but we've got work to do first thing in the morning."

"Yeah, it's late. Now that you're alive, I'm gonna go home. Get some sleep." Stye was already moving to the door. "You gonna meet me at the station in the morning?"

"Nope," Lila answered. "George and I have a stop to make. After that I'll be coming in, though. See what you can dig up by then."

"Yeah, yeah. I'll poke my nose around. See what I can sniff up." He was halfway through the door. "G'night."

The door closed before she could reply.

"He's not the most social fella I've ever met," George commented.

Lila smiled. She looked down at the clothes on her body. Ill-fitting pants and a shirt too big in some areas, and too small in others.

"These yours?" She tugged on the shirt.

"Yeah. Sorry, that was all I had," George answered.

"I appreciate it." She took a long drag on the cigarette. "So, you put them on me?"

"I…um, yes. Sorry." George looked at the ground. "Your suit was torn up, and I didn't want you to—"

"It's okay, George," she said. "I don't mind a bit."

He looked at every corner of the room, each time angling away from her. "I suppose you could stay on the couch if you want. Or you can take my bed and I'll sleep out here. That's probably the better choice."

"Or we can both take the bed. We've done it before," Lila suggested.

"No!" George's eyes snapped up to her. "No, that's okay. You just go on and take the bed. I'll take the couch."

"If you say so," Lila answered, "but the bed is a lot softer."

"That's okay. I'm good."

"I don't doubt that," Lila mumbled.

"What?" George asked.

"I said before bed I want to go get some cigarettes. Is there a store nearby?" she asked.

"Not one that's open this late. You're gonna have to wait until morning." George walked to the door and turned the lock. She watched his every step. "Sorry."

"No worries, George. I'll find something to take it's place until then." Lila licked her lips.

"Why don't I make you something to eat." George walked up to her with a smile. "You've got to be starving."

She took a deep breath and smiled back. "You're too nice, George. Thanks. Food sounds great."

"Okay. Sit. I'll whip something up."

He walked out of the room and Lila sat back down on the couch. Pain shot through her backside. And she decided that food and bed wasn't such a bad idea after all.

Chapter Fourteen

"Are you sure you wanna get out here, lady?"

"I think this will do, yes." Pussy handed over another bill to the hack driver. "Thank you for your help."

"Yeah, well, don't be too thankful." He shoved the money into his shirt pocket. The moment Pussy closed the door, the cab rolled away.

It would be wrong to call the area dark. The constant flashing from the neon behind her made the area anything but, actually. A better description in her mind was shady.

As she turned to the building, the rest of the street took on a new life. Conversations began to fill the air. People overlooked during the day openly made their way down the street.

The word flashed overhead once more. Hotel. The sign beside the door was a little more specific. It read "26th Street Variety Inn."

Fortunately, the door was unlocked. As she stepped inside, she got an instant taste for one type of variety it offered. The smells were numerous and overwhelming.

"We don't want trouble here." A voice filled the room but no one was there to own it.

"I'm not looking for trouble," Pussy answered.

"The way you look, I can't be sure it's not looking for you."

Pussy glanced down. A ragged dress and blood stains were not a good look. "It's been a long night. I'm just looking for a place to sleep."

"Who's after you?" She narrowed the location of the voice down to one of the two doors on the west wall.

"No one. I just ran into a problem that refused to go away." Pussy walked to the doors. "Are you going to let me see you now?"

The one on her left opened a crack. "You got a fella who's been beatin' on you?" It was a man's voice. He sounded small.

"More than one, actually." She allowed herself a smile. "It's okay, I give as good as I get."

"And they're not coming after you?" he asked.

"They don't know where to find me. I was told this was a place where people could just disappear."

"Everyone who comes here disappears." The door opened wider. The voice didn't match the man. He stood half a head taller than Pussy, and weighed probably five times more. His hair was greasy and the buttoned up shirt—missing two buttons—was a poor fit at best. "It's two bucks a night. Five bucks for no questions."

She handed him a twenty. "I just need one night. Do you have a room with a bath?"

He stared at the bill in his hand. "Sure. Sure, that's no problem. I got a great room for you."

"So long as it has a bath," she repeated.

He fumbled at the board beside the door. The sound of several keys ringing against each other grew until he emerged with a single offering. "This is for room 310. Best room in the place."

"Thank you." She took the key from his hand. Before she could even turn to walk away she stopped herself. "I don't suppose there is a phone in that room?"

"Not one that works. If you gotta make a call, you can use the phone in the booth there." He pointed to a door leading to a darkened room. The letters "p" and "o" were barely visible on the scratched glass. "Ring for the operator. She'll patch you through. Better call before 10:00, though. Sometimes the operator don't pick up after that."

"Thanks again." She hit the stairs and he closed the door. It was a short walk up the two floors. She took each step as quickly as she could without running.

Her room was everything she imagined it might be. There was a bed. There was even a pair of small tables on either side of it. Beyond that, she felt lucky to have blinds over the window.

The door leading out of the room was her primary interest at the moment. She looked beyond it. It wasn't a model of cleanliness, but she didn't care. It was a bathtub. She stepped in and turned the hot water on and corked the drain.

Her shoes rattled across the floor as she kicked them off, and the bed groaned under her weight. A couple of quick bounces were enough to test its quality.

The dress peeled off her, and she lay it across the foot of the bed. Faint hints of steam began to work their way into the bedroom and she rose with them. Her undergarments didn't even make it onto the bed.

"Ohhhhhh." The word poured out of her as she sank into the bath. Her left hand rested on the side of the tub while her right one swirled through the water. The soap was small and smelled like she expected. It didn't stop her from removing as much of the night's grime as she could.

With that done she rinsed and stretched out as far as the tub allowed. She laid her head back and closed her eyes.

She saw Coney. Images of them together many years back. A day when the thermometer threatened to pop from the heat, and they endured in underwear and ice cream. Sharing birthday celebrations with a cake made from leftover pancakes from their waitressing jobs. Talking until dawn about the future, the past, and surviving the present. Each of them talking about their home before they met. Neither of them speaking in fond terms. Pussy spoke of a youth with no friends. Coney reminisced about the cabin the orphanage sent her to each summer. They laughed. They cried. She saw Coney exactly as she remembered her.

And then she saw her lying on the floor. Her one brown eye-patch exposed. Then the Fizz inspired vision of her at the foot of a bed, hidden in shadow.

Her eyes popped open and she sat up, pushing water over the side of the tub. "Coney," she whispered. "No. Please, no."

The water drained from her like rain as she stepped out and grabbed the nearest towel. It was small and coarse and she didn't care. Her foot nearly slipped on the cheap tile, but she kept going.

The folded dress on the bed stopped her for a moment. It was filthy and she was fresh from the tub. "Dammit." She pushed her vanity to one side and then slipped the dress over her head.

She was still pulling on her shoes as she walked towards the stairs. The phone room at the bottom still sat empty, and she wasted no time moving into it. It looked like it was cleaned once every solar eclipse. Or maybe every other one.

The phone sparked to life but she heard nothing but faint static. A glance at her wrist showed half-past ten. "No, no, no. You stayed. Pick up the line." She jiggled the hook three times.

"How may I direct your call?" The operator sounded as though she would prefer to be pulling out her eyebrow hairs one at a time.

"Liberty 6-5476." Pussy rattled off. "Please."

There were three clicks, and then it began to ring.

"Hello." His voice was warm, welcoming, and everything she wanted to hear.

"Hello, George," Pussy replied.

"Pussy?" His voice turned to a whisper. "Thank goodness. Are you okay? I've been so worried. It's wonderful hearing your voice."

Her heart fluttered. "I feel the same. It's been a rough couple of days. Tonight especially, what with being thrown off a building and everything."

"What? Where are you?" The volume went way up.

"I'm safe. There's a…well, I hate to use the word hotel, but technically I think that's accurate." She looked through the window at what passed for a lobby. "I think it's best I don't tell you where."

"Why not?" He went back to a whisper.

"That way you won't come try to find me." She shifted in her seat. "Besides, I need you to take a message to someone."

"Who?" he asked.

"I don't know her name. It's the detective who was…." She pictured them together outside the Kit Kat Klub. "The detective working my case."

"I…what did you want to tell her?"

"You might want to write it down," Pussy suggested. "There are a few things on the list."

"I might not need to," George muttered.

"Why not?" Pussy sat up a little straighter.

"She's here." There was a long pause. She didn't interrupt it. "I can put her on the phone, if you want."

"What's she doing there?" Pussy asked.

"I brought her here. It's a long story. The short version is that she's got the cops after her now. Some of them, anyway," George said. "She's on your side, Pussy."

Her fingers strummed across the door. "If you trust her, George, then I will, too."

"You want me to put her on the phone?" he asked.

"I suppose I do." Her hand closed into a fist.

"Hold on."

"George, I…." The sound on the other end of the phone muffled. "George?"

He was gone. She felt her stomach attempt to flip over.

"Hello?" Her voice was rougher than Pussy expected.

"Good evening, Detective." She smoothed her voice out in response.

"Miss Katnip. How nice to hear from you." She was calm at least.

"I'm afraid you do have me at a bit of a disadvantage. I never did get your name," Pussy stated.

"Ringtail. Detective Lila Ringtail." She said her name with practiced precision. "I'd be happy to give you the full introduction in person."

"Not just yet," Pussy answered. "There are still a few things that I need to take care of."

"I'm not planning on arresting you, Miss Katnip. I know you didn't have anything to do with Miss Hase's death." She confirmed what George stated.

Pussy went straight to the truth. "I'm not sure that's entirely accurate, Detective. I didn't kill her, but I'm starting to think that there is something more to her death. And that I'm somehow involved."

"And just how do you figure that?" Lila asked.

"Coney came to me the other night. There was a reason for it. I just have to figure out what and why." She put the pieces into place. They fit together a little too well.

"All right, then. So, why did you want to talk to me?" Directly to the point on her side, too. Pussy smiled.

"Because I need your help," Pussy replied. "Are you familiar with the name Conner Drago?"

"Rich guy in Big City. Makes sure his name is in the social column regularly. Owns a pretty fancy hotel. That Conner Drago?" She was smart, too.

"That would be him, yes. I also think he's connected with Coney's death."

There was a hesitation. Pussy either surprised her or upset her. "That's a pretty tall order. Why would someone like him be interested in her?"

"And now we've come to what I need help with," Pussy stated. "Can you look into that? Find out what Coney has been doing for the past few years?"

"You're thinking there's something specific there. Care to share what it is?" The detective was still working. If she ever quit.

"I don't have specifics, Detective. I'll let you know when I do." Pussy couldn't answer her. Not yet.

"Assuming I agree," Lila answered, "how would I get ahold of you again?"

"I'll call George. Can you keep in touch with him?" Pussy asked.

"Oh, I'm pretty sure I can stay near George, sure." The tone in the detective's voice cause Pussy to pull the phone away for a moment.

"Okay…." She brought it back to her ear. "Oh, can you also check into another man. Goes by the name of Neko Mata. I think he may be foreign."

"Who's that?"

"One of Drago's henchman. I spotted him at the sight of the murder," Pussy explained.

"You think he's the one who poisoned her?"

What did she say? "Poisoned? What do you mean?"

"We got the tests back. Our victim was poisoned."

Pussy almost dropped the phone. She stared straight ahead but didn't see anything. "Oh, Coney. Why?"

"Miss Katnip?" Pussy heard the detective calling her.

"I'm here." Pussy brought the phone back. "Did you happen to notice the overturned furniture?"

"Sure. I figured that happened in the fight," Lila answered.

"What fight?" Pussy asked.

"The one that you had while you were there. I'm guessing it was probably with this Mata character."

She hadn't mentioned the fight. It was a good idea to watch what she said around this woman.

"You're good, Detective."

"That's what they tell me," she answered.

"I didn't touch the furniture. It was like that when I got there. Coney…" the name caught in her throat, "the victim's body was already on the floor. Mata was standing over her, looking straight at me when I entered. I had assumed she was in a struggle with him, but now…."

"Now you're wondering if the furniture wasn't already overturned when he got there." Lila finished her thought.

"Someone was looking for something. I think I know what. Or at least the owner of the item. Can you do a once-over on the place?" Pussy asked.

"Sure. I don't have anything better to do." The phone dripped from the detective's tone.

"Sorry, Detective, but I don't think I'm welcome there right now." One good attitude deserved another.

"You're not welcome anywhere. Watch your back, Miss Katnip. Some police might be out to do you in."

The detective's voice was deep and clear. No undertone of anything. "Thanks for the warning. You might want to watch out, too. Drago has worked his way into the force, as I hear it."

"Really?" She could hear the woman's eyebrow raise. "Now that is information I can do something with."

"My pleasure," Pussy answered. "Can you put George back on the line?"

"Are we done?" the detective asked.

"Unless you have something else, yes. Don't worry, you'll be hearing from me."

"Until then, Miss Katnip."

"It was a pleasure…." The tone of the receiver changed. "Hello?"

And that was it. Detective Lila Ringtail didn't even wait for a good-bye. Pussy felt it was for the best.

"Pussy?" George's voice brought the warmth back to her ear.

"I'm sorry, George," she said.

"Sorry? For what?" he replied.

"The fact that I'm not there. That I won't…that I can't tell you where to find me." Pussy held the next words inside for a moment. "I could use you beside me right now."

"Are you okay, Pussy?"

She wanted to scream into the phone. Tell him the truth. Instead, she just said, "I'm fine."

He didn't answer. So she spoke again.

"George, I think I know what happened to Coney. I don't want to say what. Not until I have proof. I…I need you to do something for me." Pussy wiped her hand on the tattered remains of her dress.

"Of course, Pussy. Whatever you need." She could tell he meant it.

"You have to find her body. I need you to check something for me." Pussy felt her shoulders tighten up. "Can you do that?"

"What?" His whisper was forceful. "Why?"

"Why isn't important. Not right now. Are you willing to do it?" The lump in her throat grew three sizes.

"Yes. Of course I will, Pussy." His words were more soothing than his tone. "What am I doing?"

She laid it out for him. Exactly what she needed. It wasn't difficult, but it was disturbing.

"That doesn't make sense, Pussy," he said.

"I know it doesn't. And I hope I'm wrong, but…can you do it anyway?"

"I will. If I can. I promise." He sounded like George again. Her shoulders relaxed.

"Thank you, George. I…." The words ran through her mind. "I hope to see you soon."

"Me too, Pussy. I'd tell you to take care of yourself, but you're already the best I've ever seen at taking care of everything. Including yourself."

"You're the best, George." Pussy smiled.

"No, I just said that title belongs to you. I'll talk to you soon, Pussy," George said.

"Tomorrow. I'll call around dinner time," she said. "Take care, George."

She listened until the line went dead. After placing the receiver back she left the booth and headed up to her room.

The dress came off. She folded it up a second time.

"And the first thing I get to do tomorrow is buy some new clothes." She tossed the dress onto the floor. "Again."

Pussy crawled onto the bed and waited for sleep to come.

Chapter Fifteen

"So, what are we hoping to find?"

Lila waited until George was inside and she had the door closed before answering. "We'll know when we find it."

"That's not a helpful answer." George's progress stopped at the body outline on the floor.

"Trust me, if I had a better answer I'd give it to you." Lila stepped beside him. "Ignore that. It's just a marker, anyway."

"I know. I've found dead people before. The difference is that a fire doesn't try to kill someone." George looked away. "I thought you already searched this place."

"The forensic people gave it the thorough once-over. I just came through and hit the highlights, so to speak." She moved over to the couch and walked from one end of it to the other.

"So, what's the deal with you and Katnip?" she asked.

"Pussy? We're friends. Good friends." George stood over by the window, watching her. "Why?"

"Must be very good friends. It's not common to see a fugitive trust someone enough to call them at their house." Lila looked inside the bedroom where she spoke with the neighbor last time here. "Or conversely come to the fugitive's aid at the drop of a hat."

"Pussy's not guilty. You know that," George answered.

"True. That doesn't change her status, though. You could get in serious trouble for helping her out. It could cost you your career." Lila walked to the kitchen door and looked inside.

"She'd do the same for me."

When she looked at him, George stood with his arms crossed over his chest.

"I have no doubt." Lila pulled out a cigarette and struck a match. "Thanks again for stopping to pick up a new deck."

"You're welcome. Why are you asking about Pussy?" George prodded.

The warmth of the smoke radiated through her chest. After a moment she let it out in a steady breath. "I've been about as subtle as a wrecking ball, George. Don't tell me you haven't noticed."

"I…." George couldn't get past a single word.

"Just tell me if I'm wasting my time." Lila cut to the chase.

He swallowed. "I can't answer that."

The smoke rolled out of the corners of Lila's mouth as they turned upwards. "Good enough."

"What, um…." George cleared his throat with a half-cough. "Why did we come back here? I know Pussy suggested it, but I still don't understand why."

She pulled the cigarette out of her mouth and held it between the first two fingers on her right hand. It made for a convenient pointer. "First time through, I thought we were looking at a struggle. According to Miss Katnip, the room was torn up when she got here." Lila walked to stand beside the outline on the floor, facing the front door. "Which meant that someone else did it. Miss Katnip also said that the presumed assailant was standing over the body right here." She pointed to the door. "Facing this way."

"Yeah, okay." George stepped a little closer.

"What do you see about this?" Her hand gestured towards the outline. She watched George's mind processing the scene.

"I don't know," he answered.

"She's sideways to me." Lila pointed to the head of the outline and followed to her feet. "If I was attacking her, wouldn't it make sense that either she would fall away from me or towards me? Falling down to the side seems a bit odd."

"Maybe she fell straight and the attacker moved around to stand beside her," George suggested. "Why is this important?"

"When I was here before, I checked the victim's fingernails. Nothing. The nails were perfect. Painted even. Not a scratch on them." Lila stepped over the outline. "The victim was a slight thing. If she was gonna fight, there'd be a lot of scratching involved."

"So you don't think she fought against whoever Pussy found here?" George turned his head to look around the room.

"And the door wasn't broken when Katnip arrived. The neighbor says she busted it in. I'm trusting that Katnip is smart enough to try a door knob first. That means the door was locked from the inside." Lila walked to the window. Wood was nailed up over the broken pane.

173

"Which means that the person who fought Pussy was let into the apartment." George's mouth hung open. "Coney knew him."

"Yep. Katnip suggested that whoever created this mess was looking for something." She pointed to the body outline. "And if our assailant was still dealing with the woman on the floor, he either found what he was looking for, hadn't started looking for it yet, or wasn't looking for anything at all."

"But if he didn't make the mess, then who did?" George asked.

"That's what you and I get to figure out." She moved to the broken furniture. "We can assume that they either found what they wanted or discovered that it wasn't here."

"How do you know that?" George asked.

Lila walked back to the center of the room. "Because they haven't been back. This is exactly what the place looked like the last time I was here."

"That…makes perfect sense." The hint of amazement in George's voice brought a new smile to her face.

"Well, we're done here. We need to go by my apartment for a minute. Mind driving me home?" Lila asked.

"I'm not going to leave you alone, Lila," George answered.

"I certainly hope not," she replied.

"Why are we going by your place?" he asked.

"Two things. First, as cute as your clothes look on me, they aren't right for me heading to the precinct. Second, there's something that I need to have checked out. I meant to give it to the forensic people yesterday, but it slipped my mind. I guess I had something else at home that kept my attention."

George cleared his throat sharply. "What is it?" He went to the front door and opened it.

"That is exactly what I want to know." Lila stepped past him and into the hall.

The huff from behind her said as much as his next words. "Do you ever give a straight answer?"

She looked at him. "I think it's the poison, George. I won't know until the lab can check it out and compare it to whatever killed her."

"What? Let's get over there." George hurried down the stairs. She followed close behind.

The drive over to her place was mostly quiet. Filled with thinking more than talking. George's eyes were watching the road, but his mind seemed focused elsewhere. Lila decided not to ask exactly where. She did speak before they got to her apartment.

"Don't park right in front. Just in case," she suggested.

"You're worried there might be more cops there looking for you?" George pulled the car over to the curb.

"Exactly." She opened the door to the car. "You can wait here. I should be back in a few minutes."

"No." He opened his own door. "I'm this far in. I'm not about to leave you alone now."

"Why George, aren't you the gentleman." The teasing tone hid the sincerity as much as she could manage.

"I'm just wanting you safe," he countered.

She smiled and led him around the corner, towards the door to her building. Four cars were parked along the road. Three of them she recognized. The fourth was new. There appeared to be no occupants.

"Keep your eyes open, George," she whispered.

"Did you see something?" His head started turning to either side as they walked.

"Just something out of place. Might be nothing." The doorway to the building was empty and unlocked. Lila paused inside the door and held a finger to her mouth. George took the hint and stayed silent. The building was only slightly younger than the earth it sat on. The floorboards creaked at the slightest step. Her head turned to the side, listening.

"Okay." The lack of sound was good enough. "Let's go."

She wasted no time going up the floors to her apartment. A turn of the lock and they had entrance inside. She shut the door and locked it behind her.

"Are we acting a little paranoid?" George asked.

"Probably." Lila walked towards her room. She began to unbutton the borrowed shirt on the third step. "But it's better to be safe."

George spun around to stare at the door. "Well, uh, I guess I'll wait here while you change."

"What, you don't like me like I am any more?" she teased. "Besides, it's not like there's anything you haven't already seen."

"That was different," he mumbled to the door. "I'll…I'll just wait here."

"Suit yourself. I'll go pin some diapers on." She stepped into the bedroom as she pulled off the shirt. The belt and pants followed soon enough.

The closet opened, revealing her wardrobe. One suit. The only clean one of the three she owned. Two now, she supposed. At least her shoes were still intact. And George was kind enough to loan her the outfit that got her there. She softly bit her lower lip while an idea formed.

"Hey George," she shouted while fastening her pants, "I was thinking. I'm going to keep this outfit. The one you gave me, I mean. I'll have it cleaned. It's the least I can do, since you were so kind about letting me wear it. I'd hate to give you your rags back that had my smell all over it." She paused. "Unless you want that, I mean."

The next room over remained silent.

"Don't worry, George," she stepped to the door as she buttoned the shirt, "I promise not to—"

She cut herself off and launched into the room. A man had George pinned against the front door. One arm was across George's throat. George clawed at the arm, trying to pull it free.

Another man stood between Lila and George. The nightstick in his hand didn't deter her at all. His swing came from overhead. She slipped to her right and drove her left shoulder into him. It drove him back, but not off his feet.

The nightstick came down again, this time connecting with her back. Pain shot through her entire body, but she moved on. Driving forward past him towards the man restraining George. Towards the nightstick hanging from his waist.

With a yank she pulled it off him. As the man turned to look at her, she brought the stick around in a sideways motion. A sound reminiscent of a melon breaking open preceded him falling to the ground in a heap.

George gasped for air. That was good enough. Lila turned just in time to see the nightstick heading towards her face.

Years of practiced reflexes turned her away and brought her own stick up. The sharp clack of the sticks meeting rang in her ears. The impact of her nightstick on his was enough to deflect the blow somewhat, but it still hit her cheek with enough force to leave a nasty bruise in the morning.

That was all she was going to allow.

She drove the end of her nightstick into his solar plexus. He doubled over, grabbing hold of her waist and pushing her back against the wall. She heard her nightstick clatter to the floor and slide away from her.

Her left arm wrapped around the man's neck, pinning his head to her hip. One after another, she drove her right hand into his side. She could feel him lurch against her with each punch.

Then she felt him grab her legs and pull up. She fell onto her back, and he crashed on top of her. He reared up, pulling his fist back beside his shoulder. Lila's hand flashed up and drove into his throat. Both of his hands went to his neck, and his eyes bulged from their sockets.

Another sickening sound struck behind him, and he collapsed on top of her. He was dead weight.

"Get off of me!" Lila shoved upward and turned to the side. She rolled away and the man fell back to the floor.

George loomed behind him on one knee. The nightstick in his hand rested partially on the floor.

"Sorry," he wheezed. "They got on me before I could make a sound."

"Not your fault." Lila pushed and pulled herself up to a standing position. "I should have checked the whole house when we got here."

George stood up and rolled his neck around once. "It's okay. We're both a little off today." He nodded towards them. "What are we going to do with them? Are they alive?"

"Yeah. They'll need to go to the hospital, though." She moved over to her phone. "I'll call the ambulance."

"Do you know these guys?" he asked.

"Never seen them in my life. I have an idea where they're from, though." She picked up the other nightstick off the floor. "And we're going to keep hold of these, just in case."

"That was pretty impressive," George said.

"What?" Lila paused as she lifted the receiver.

"You. Fighting those two." He rubbed his neck.

"Thanks." She jiggled the hook a few times. "You should see me in heels."

The phone clicked and she heard a voice on the other side. "Operator, this is Detective Lila Ringtail of the MTPD. I need an ambulance sent to the following address…."

Chapter Sixteen

All she could do was sit and wait. And it was driving her nuts.

The difference between the high-end dresses she saw yesterday and the second hand shop with few things in her size stood worlds apart. Today she didn't care about the fashion. She just wanted something that fit. And a hat. Particularly, a large hat.

After that, she made her way back to the scene of the crime, so to speak. A long walk from the second hand and a cab ride downtown brought her to the neighborhood. She told him to drop her at the cafe down the street. From there it was a short stroll right to the hotel.

So, all she had to do was wait until the time was right. After two hours, it was becoming excruciating.

"Can I warm that up for you, honey?" The waitress made a point to drop by every five minutes or so to remind Pussy that she had been sitting in that seat for some time now. Not that Pussy blamed her.

"Please." Pussy smiled. "And I'll take another of those pastries you brought me before."

"You didn't eat the last one." The waitress filled the coffee cup in front of Pussy. "You sure you want one?"

There was a soft sound as the bill slid to the edge of the table. "No, I don't really, but I figure I need to buy something to sit here. Will this cover it?"

The waitress's hand drifted across the table and the bill disappeared. "You enjoy your coffee, honey."

Pussy picked up the cup and inhaled the aroma. The bitterness mixed with a nutty chocolate undertone was almost enough to keep her awake. A few sips of the strong brew were enough to guarantee it.

People were creatures of habit. It was one of the few truisms that Pussy believed with all her heart. Right now, she hoped Drago's arrival at the hotel yesterday wasn't an oddity.

And then, there he was.

Conner Drago, flanked by Neko Mata and Tayra. The site of Neko's arm in a sling and Tayra in a neck brace brightened her rather low mood. The trio stopped just outside the door of the hotel and lingered. They didn't have to wait long. Pussy recognized the make of the car. A Paragon L-7. One of the latest items to make it to the nouveau riche portfolio. Most people would be in awe of it. To her, it seemed like a waste of money.

All three men crawled into the vehicle and it pulled away from the front of the Velvet Arms. She waited an extra minute after it was out of sight, and took one last sip of coffee. Then she freed up the booth for the waitress.

The traffic was light, and the walk easy. Approaching the door, her hand pulled the brim of her hat a little lower. She stepped inside the hotel and immediately turned to her right, away from the front desk.

The entrance to the stairs was tucked away, which couldn't have made her happier. It was a long walk up to the sixteenth floor, but that gave her time to consider how to reach the seventeenth. Julian mentioned something about many of Drago's employees living there. She would just have to be careful to avoid Julian himself.

The sixteenth floor looked a lot like the fifth floor. The room numbers were different, but the pattern was the same. Minus the fact that the stairwell ended here. Somewhere, somehow, there had to be a passage up. Unless there was a unique set of stairs leading from the lobby to the seventeenth and eighteenth floor, the people one flight up had to have a way down here.

She paced the hallway. Walking to one end and then back to the other. Every door was in place. Nothing was different. From the corner suite to the storage closet to the garbage chute, everything was exactly like it was eleven floors lower.

A glance at her wrist showed that almost twenty minutes were gone from the time that Drago and his goons had left the Velvet Arms. She had no idea when he would be back. Time was rapidly turning into her enemy. Without thinking she slammed her fist into the wall. The opening to the garbage chute rattled.

Pussy stopped. The ten feet she walked stretched down the hallway. The tinny squeak from the hinge showed the wear of the garbage chute. She stuck her hand in and held it still. The faintest hint of a breeze wafted past it. If she remembered correctly, all these chutes had to go all the way to the roof to allow the gases to vent. Which meant it went up as well as down.

The first thing to go was the hat. Then she peeled off her heels and threw them down the chute after it. Her hand went back in and traveled the full width of the shaft.

"Two feet," she mumbled. "Maybe a little more, but not much."

Her hand went into a pocket and pulled out three vials of red liquid. She popped the top off of one vial of Fizz and downed the contents.

The hallway changed. The ceiling flew upwards, and the floor fell away. She hung in the air, suspended by nothing. She looked down. Faint images raced by below her.

A thin man in a bright white suit stumbled. A fat man in a deep blue suit followed behind, pushing a broom. She glanced up. Three dolls dangled by a string, staring down at the men below. Above them, a figure held all three strings, hidden in shadow.

Pussy's feet stumbled as the floor and ceiling returned. The wall beside her was enough support to keep her upright. And a second later she was able to stand on her own. The feeling of her heart pounding and her blood racing sent a tingle through her body.

A quick shake of her head cleared the rest of the cobwebs away. Gripping the hem of her skirt, she pulled apart, ripping a tear halfway up her thigh. She repeated the same action on the other side.

The door to the garbage chute was much more narrow than the chute beyond. And along with that, it opened at an odd angle. Neither of these things caused a moment's hesitation.

Pussy put first one leg and then the other into the opening. Her feet dangled down the shaft, feeling for the sides. A film of some sort covered the metal walls, and Pussy did her best not to think about its origin.

Her hands let go and she slid down the chute. Immediately she pressed her feet out to the sides and her hands in front of her, pushing her back against the rear of the chute. It took a couple of feet, but her fall stopped.

The first sense that came to her was the smell. Rancid waste mixed with something sickly sweet to create an odor uniquely its own. Her eyes watered. Bile grew at the back of her throat. She made it stop right there.

She looked up. A dot of light glistened in the distance. The vent to the roof. Probably thirty, maybe forty feet. If she was guessing correctly, she wouldn't need to go anywhere near that far. A glance down revealed darkness. She almost smiled at the conflicted feelings of uncertain danger and comforting lack of depth.

Her hands pressed against the chute, holding her in place while her feet worked their way up and pushed into the sides. Then she let her feet push her up and her hands catch her before anything else slipped. A journey of almost four inches.

Repeating it again and again, Pussy made her way up the chute. The time factor wormed its way back into her head, but she wasn't in any position to change it at the moment.

One more look up spotted a glimpse of light in the shaft wall. Another opening. This one for the seventeenth floor. At least she hoped it was.

There was the familiar squeak of the hinge as she pushed the chute doorway open. She wondered if the space beyond was actually another hallway. If not, that created problems all their own.

Like a perverted birth, she wormed her way out of the opening. At first she pulled, and then pushed against the door until she was completely free from the shaft.

The hallway stretched in two directions.

"And now to find the right door." Her eyes became slits. "On the first try. And before anyone comes out into the hall."

She let out a long, steady breath and headed down the hallway. It didn't take long to reach the end of the passage, and the large window letting light flood inside.

On the way, Pussy counted both doors and steps. Unlike the floors below, each door on this floor was inset from the hall, creating a shallow entryway outside each. Though there were fewer than on the lower floors, each door was equidistant. At least on this side of the hall. Chances were good that the rooms were the same.

And there were five doors on either side of the corridor. Ten doors in total. Considering the person she was looking for, the chances were better that she was on this side of building.

Pussy went to the first door on the right and inhaled deeply. Nothing. Across the hall she did the same. Still nothing. The process repeated. Going to a door. Inhaling deeply. Then moving to the next.

On the fifth door she found what she wanted.

All of Pussy's senses were somewhat heightened by the Fizz, and the faint smell of clove was just noticeable outside this door. The exact same clove scent she noticed on Desiree when they met.

She tried the door knob, and was pleasantly surprised when it opened. The door swung silently open and closed behind her as she rushed into the room. The deep shadows in the room blinded her long enough to stop her in the entryway. Less than a minute later she was able to see.

The room was small, but larger than a normal room in the hotel. Just past the entry was a small kitchen, then an equally small living space. The remainder of the space was hidden behind a dense curtain that spanned the width of the room.

The carpet had little cushion to it, but it was enough to muffle her steps. Her hand slipped through the gap in the curtain, letting a sliver of dim light through. A bed waited on the other side, and the person she wanted to see lay curled up on top of it.

Padding over to the bed, Pussy slipped onto it and gently pressed her hand over Desiree's mouth. The woman woke with a start, screaming into the palm over her mouth.

"Shh." Pussy whispered. "Relax. I'm not going to hurt you."

Her eyes darted back and forth, but Pussy felt the woman's breath come under control.

"Are you calm now?" Pussy asked.

Desiree nodded.

Pussy kept the gap between her hand and the other woman's mouth small. "Do you remember me?"

"Of course," Desiree whispered. "What are you doing here? How are you here?"

"I wanted to talk to you," she replied. "I need some answers."

"I…I don't know what I could say of any importance." Desiree sat up. She was naked. At least down to her waist.

Pussy turned her head. "Would you like to put something on?"

"Hmm? Oh. I…we don't normally…that is I haven't been given any clothes for the day."

Pussy's head came back around. "What does that mean?"

"That Mr. Drago hasn't decided what to do with me today. Not yet." Desiree pulled the sheets up in front of her body.

"Hasn't decided what—" Pussy caught her voice rising and stopped. "Desiree, last night you tried to warn me. Told me to run. Did you know what was going to happen."

Her head shook side to side. "I just wanted you to be free."

Pussy's tongue pressed into her right fang. "You're not free?"

"No, ma'am." She shook her head again. "At least…. I have to stay with Mr. Drago. I am in great debt to him, and if I were to try to leave, my family would be paying for it. Possibly with their lives."

A warm taste of iron filled the back of Pussy's mouth. "He is keeping you as a…." She couldn't finish. "You were worried that was going to happen to me."

Desiree's nod was almost imperceptible.

"How many people has he done this to?" she asked.

"I do not know. There are at least eight of us here. Six women and two men. We aren't allowed to speak to each other without one of our superiors around." Desiree hung her head. "Or we are punished."

The sound of cloth tearing caused Desiree to jump in surprise. Pussy looked down to see her hand filled with the bedspread and a large rip beside it.

"And what does he make you do?" Pussy growled.

"Whatever he needs. Each of us is working off our debt to him. And he is teaching us valuable skills." Desiree held her head high. "I have learned much about being a skilled bartender."

"And how long will it take to…pay him back?" A tightness worked its way through Pussy's neck.

"I do not know. I'm sorry, ma'am. We aren't told that information." She pointed towards the side wall. "Mr. Perro is in charge of debt and restoration."

"Is he?" The image of Julian's face burned in Pussy's mind.

"Yes, ma'am."

"Desiree," Pussy eased the words out, "did you know a woman named Coney?"

Her eyes moved to stare at the bed. "No. No, I do not know that name, I'm sorry."

Many thoughts raced through Pussy's mind. She pushed the violent ones to the side. For now. "Desiree, is there another way out of here besides the elevator?"

"Yes, ma'am." Again she pointed. "The emergency stairs are just past the elevator door."

"Where do they lead?"

"To the floor below. In case of emergency we are to go to them and exit down. They come out in an empty room. We exit that room and go to the main stairway to leave."

"That's why I couldn't see them," Pussy mumbled.

"Ma'am?" Desiree turned her head slightly.

"Nothing." Pussy looked around the room. "Isn't there anything for you to wear?"

"No, ma'am." She shook her head again.

"Getting you out of here is going to be a challenge then." Pussy stood up from the bed and held out her hand.

"Getting out?" Desiree's eyes turned to pale blue saucers. "No! I can't. If they caught me…." She shook her head. "And even if they didn't catch me, the others would suffer as an example."

Pussy watched as the woman almost trembled at her own words. "I'm going to break every bone in his body," she snarled.

"Do not try, ma'am." Desiree urged. "Please. He is…. There is a curse on that man. He is not normal."

"What do you mean?" Pussy raised an eyebrow.

"They say…" Desiree looked around the otherwise empty room, "…they say he cannot be killed. That death only makes him reborn again."

"Well then, that's not a problem," Pussy answered. "I didn't say I was going to kill him."

It was hard to see in the dim light, but Pussy was fairly sure that Desiree's lips twitched in a suppressed laugh.

"Desiree, I need to get up there. Does that staircase lead up as well?" she asked.

"No, ma'am. Only down. I have only gone up by the elevator," Desiree said.

"Then going up there is going to be rather noticeable." Pussy tapped her chin.

"Not if you go tonight," Desiree answered. "There will be many people visiting Mr. Drago tonight."

"Why do you say that?" Pussy asked.

"A man of some importance is arriving. Mr. Drago has arranged a party in his honor. I am supposed to be there as well. I'm hoping as a bartender," Desiree explained.

The smile on Pussy's lips grew wide. "Then I'm going to see you tonight, Desiree. And this time, plan on leaving with me. Debt paid in full."

"You…you would do that for me?" Her voice was almost a breath.

"Not just you." Pussy's eyes narrowed. "Everyone. Mr. Drago is going to have a bad night."

"But how are you—"

"Leave that to me," Pussy cut her off. "The tricky part is going to be finding an invitation to get me into the party in the first place."

"I cannot help you there, ma'am," Desiree said.

"It's alright. I have some connections." Pussy smiled. "I'm going to help, Desiree. I'll be at the party. I promise."

"I believe you." Desiree smiled, but her face quickly turned sour. "If I can say so, ma'am. I also suggest you shower. You smell like garbage."

"I don't doubt it," Pussy replied. "Which is why I'm grateful you know where the stairs are. I'll see you tonight."

Desiree nodded. Pussy turned and walked to the door. Then the hall. Then the stairs leading down.

Chapter Seventeen

"Don't worry about it." She shook her pack of cigarettes and did a quick count of the number left. Satisfied, she put the pack in her front pocket and took a long drag from the one between her lips.

"How am I not supposed to worry about it?" George rushed up beside her, still taking one step at a time. She was taking two. "They've already tried to kill you twice, and by association, kill me as well. Now we're walking right into the belly of the beast."

Lila glanced at him. "That's a little dramatic, don't you think?"

"You know what I mean," George grumbled.

"We've been over this, George. The least likely place for anyone to attack me is here." Lila took a final puff from the pill and tossed it to the ground. Her foot casually crushed it as she opened the door to the precinct.

"It could also be the place where you have the most people wanting to kill you gathered in one building." George took the door handle from her, holding it open.

There was no argument from her. She stepped through it with a smile on her face. "Sure, there's that possibility, too."

She stopped just inside the building.

"I can't believe your attitude. How can you be so calm?" he whispered.

"Oh, I'm not calm. I'm planning. I'll get to calm after this whole thing is over." There were five officers in her line of sight. None of them looked her way or acknowledged her at all.

"Okay, what now?" George asked.

She pulled out another cigarette. As it went to her mouth a lit match joined it. "I go to my desk. That's what I do."

"That's not what I meant," he grumbled.

"I know, but it's the truth. I go to my desk and start from there. I have to figure out who in this precinct is out to get me, which means I need to give them an obvious target." She pulled the cigarette out for a moment. "That would be at my desk."

"Fine. Where do you want me? Should I be at the desk, too?" George's head turned from one side to the other, scanning the room.

"Probably. It's up to you." Lila started walking towards the squad room. "The important thing is to act like nothing is wrong."

"They'll believe that?" George asked.

"I sure hope so." As she entered the squad room, over a dozen more officers came into view. And that didn't count the ones in the side offices. Like Lieutenant Vehrka's office.

Now people were taking notice of her. Nothing too out of the ordinary. They always liked to stare at their token as she entered the room. This time she tried to meet as many of the eyes as she could. Most of them continued to stare. A handful turned away.

Her desk was the same way she left it. The chair squeaked as she sat down. "Imagine that," she mumbled.

"What?" George sat in the chair beside her desk.

"The lieutenant still hasn't given me a new case to work on. He was supposed to get that to me yesterday." She stared across the room at his office. The blinds on his windows were closed, but light snuck between the slats.

She saw George turn his head to follow her eyes. "You think that he's…."

"Maybe. I won't be sure until I ask him." She tapped the end from her cigarette into the ashtray on the desk.

"You can't just walk over there and ask him!" George fought the volume down, making his exclamation a rather loud whisper.

She sighed. "Look, George, I'm not going to do anything stupid. I don't want you getting hurt, and I certainly don't want me getting hurt. I gotta go talk to him, though."

"You said you had to sit at your desk."

"That's true. And I'm going to for a little while. After that, I start poking." Her finger tapped the air to reinforce her words.

He just stared at her. It was obvious he was thinking, but she wasn't sure about what. She hoped it involved the two of them away from this place.

"I have to…." George gestured over his shoulder.

"Bathroom is down the hallway on the left. You can't miss it." She leaned in over her desk. "Be careful. I don't think they'll come after you, but you can't be too safe."

"Yeah. Yeah, don't worry. I'll be careful." He stood up and lingered for a moment. Then he walked away.

"Ringtail."

Stye didn't yell or even raise his voice, but the sound of her name still caused her to turn with a start. He took the chair George just vacated.

"I was doin' that checkin' on stuff. On that Drago guy, plus the Hase broad." He tapped a folder held in his other hand.

"Good morning to you, too, Stye." She pointed to the folder. "What's it say?"

"This ain't the folder on Drago." He shook his head. "This is the folder on Drago."

A thin, folded piece of manilla paper landed on her desk. Her right eyebrow pushed her hair up. "He has a folder."

"Yeah, sorta. It's an empty folder, but it's a folder."

"And what does that say?" Lila asked.

"That there ain't nothin' worth sayin' about the guy." Stye shrugged casually.

"Nope." Lila took a deep drag on her cigarette. "If there was nothing, there wouldn't be a folder. Empty says that things are missing. That everything is missing."

"Then where did it go?" Stye asked.

"That's what I intend to find out." She nodded towards him. "What about the other one?"

"Well, you ain't likely to be happy about this one, either." He put the folder on the desk. "This is about the Hase dame."

She turned it around and opened it up. One page slipped out. Three others stayed in place.

The Devil Was Green

"This it? I'm the one who put this in here." She closed it back up. "Did you look into where she was? Make some calls?"

He nodded. "Turns out she came in here sixteen days ago. Train from Harborton, which connected all the way back to The Big Apple. She got there on a plane from across the pond."

"Yeah, I thought as much. Let me guess: Europe?" she asked.

"Nah. Africa." His eyes glanced down. "So, south pond, I guess."

"Africa?" The word dragged out of her mouth. "Why would she…?" Lila looked back at Stye. "Do me another favor. Find out if Drago's been out of town in the past couple of weeks. Can you do that?"

"I guess, sure." He stood up from the chair. "What are you thinkin'?"

"Just connecting dots right now." She tapped the top of her desk. Stye started to walk away. "Oh!" He turned back. "What about that Mata fellow? Did you get anything about him?"

"Nah. Nothing." His face twisted up. "Well, nothing real."

"Go on," she urged.

"Just a stupid story one guy told me. Said that name wasn't a name. It was a…a devil or something. Some sort of Oriental legend about a thing that turns into other things." He rolled his eyes. "Like I said, nothing real."

"Thing that turns into other things? Anything more specific?" she asked.

"I dunno. A monster I think. Something about a cat with two tails. I dunno. I kinda ignored it after he got to the word devil."

Stye shrugged. "I'll go check on Drago for ya. You gonna be around for a while?"

Her eyes moved through the room, looking for anyone staring back her way. "For a little while, anyway."

"Good. I'll get back to ya." As Stye walked away, one hand was busy pulling up his pants by the belt.

Lila stood up. She just stood there, looking at the whole room from a different position behind her desk. Then she stepped around to the side. Then the front. And before she knew it, she was halfway to the lieutenant's office.

The closed blinds blocked direct vision, but they couldn't stop all the light. Shadows passed by them. The lieutenant wasn't alone.

"What are you doing, Ringtail?"

She looked at Morgan behind his desk. The more pressing need was to go in and see the lieutenant, but it was hard to fight down the urge. It shouldn't take long at all.

"Morgan." She stood across his desk from him. "How's my case going? Have you made any progress?"

"Well, I—"

"Because I think you should look into where Hase was before she was killed. Maybe see if there's some sort of connection there."

"If you—"

"Then again, you're probably still hunting for Katnip. What a shame. She had nothing to do with the murder, after all. But why look for facts when it's so much easier to just be a good pet and follow your master's orders."

"Hey! That's—"

"I'd love to stay and chat." Lila walked away from the desk. "But grown ups have to talk now."

She felt Morgan rise to his feet behind her. He wasn't a small man, but he wasn't fast enough to make him dangerous. And all he did was stand as she put her hand on the lieutenant's door.

"…mess this has become!"

The words stopped when she opened the door. Both men stared at her as she closed it behind her. The lieutenant she expected to see in the room. The other man, not so much.

"Captain Saunders." She pushed the words through her teeth. "I wasn't aware you were here today."

He didn't answer.

"What do you want, Ringtail?" the lieutenant asked.

"Oh, just checking in, Boss. I've had quite the eventful day or so. Had a car try to drive me off the road. Who knows what they would have done?" She made a bit of a show pulling out a new cigarette. The match blazed to life and shared its fire with the tip of the butt. "Oh, and then this morning two guys came to my apartment. I think they wanted to hurt me. Not sure though." She blew out a long stream of smoke. "I'll have to wait until the hospital says they can answer questions."

"We're having a conversation, Lila." Captain Saunders stated. "Maybe you can come back a little later?"

"Maybe. Depends on what's going on then." She looked back at the lieutenant. "Still waiting on that new case, Boss. Right now I've just got a lot of free time on my hands. Neither of us really wants that, do we?"

"Go back to your desk, Detective." Lieutenant Vehrka pointed straight to his door. "I'll deal with you later."

"Third time's the charm, eh?" she growled.

"What the hell is that supposed to mean?" The lieutenant shouted.

Both of her hands slammed down on his desk. "It means that I'm not going away. It doesn't matter how many goons come after me, I'm gonna be here. And you can't do a damn thing about it."

"I will not be talked to in my office that way by a damned—" He cut himself off.

"Say it! Or don't you have the stones to use that word in my face?" Lila almost crawled up onto the desk.

"By a damned 'coon!" he shouted.

Her teeth came out.

"You're lucky. If we weren't in this office I'd turn you out. Oh, and this 'coon is going to say a lot more before she's done." Lila pulled back and stood up. "I just wanted to come in and watch your face. To see your expression when you saw me."

"Lila." She turned to Captain Saunders. No emotion showed on his face. "You've made your point. Now leave."

She stared at him. "Why, Captain? You didn't need me. You probably didn't even want me. Why bring me here at all?"

He took a deep breath. "For all the right reasons. Please, Lila, go back to your desk."

She pointed a finger at him. "You're gonna have to give me answers, Captain. One way or another." Her head snapped around to the lieutenant. "Oh, and next time, don't send a flunky. If you want something done…. Well, you know the rest."

The door slammed against the jamb as she yanked it open. She stormed into the squad room. Every eye was on her. The expressions behind them were mixed.

"Lila?" George's voice was to the right and behind her. She turned her whole body that direction and met him halfway. "What was that?"

The pounding sound in her ears was starting to subside. Which was news to her, as she hadn't noticed it before it was almost gone. She inhaled a long drag and then let it out with her words. "Exactly what I told myself I wouldn't do."

"You confronted him?" George looked past her at the rest of the room.

"Yeah. I still have more of a temper than I'd like. I'm much better when I just have something to think about." She looked down and shook her head.

"Don't be too hard. I don't know many people who would even have had the guts to show up here today. I think I can count them on two fingers, actually." She felt his hand on her arm. Her whole body relaxed a touch.

"Thanks, George. I appreciate you—" Her eyes wandered to the right. Lila stopped talking. Detective Ringtail asked him a question. "George, where were you?"

"What do you mean? I was just off…." He pointed behind him.

"The bathrooms are that way." She indicated the opposite direction. "You came from over here. There isn't much down that hall. What were you doing?"

George didn't say anything. His face paled slightly.

"There are only two things that way, George. The holding cells and the morgue. Which one did you visit?" She took a half step away from him.

"The morgue," he whispered.

"Why?" If she could make it less than one syllable, she would.

He shifted his weight. She stayed steady.

"Pussy asked me to," he admitted.

Her eyes bore into his until he had to turn them away. "I'm waiting. Tell me more."

"I can't." He looked back up at her. "After I talk to Pussy I'll tell you everything if she doesn't, but I told her I wouldn't tell anyone else until I spoke with her."

Lila felt the heat rising from inside. "If you are betraying me, George…."

"I'm not!" His answer was instantaneous. "I won't do anything to hurt you, Lila. I swear."

And just like that, her anger softened. She wanted to fume about it, but there was no way to deny his sincerity. "You better not," she mumbled.

Without another word she turned and stalked across the room back to her desk. George was only two steps behind her.

"So, what now?" George asked.

The phone on Lila's desk rang.

"MTPD, Detective Ringtail." The answer was completely rote.

She wasn't expecting the voice on the other end. "Good day, Detective," Pussy said. "I trust you've been busy?"

"You could call it that. Why are you calling here? I thought you were phoning us later today." Lila moved up on her chair and leaned into the desk.

"That would be too late," Pussy stated. "I think it's time we meet. I know what we need to do."

Chapter Eighteen

"You look stunning."

This was a serious moment. She understood the circumstances and the weight of it. That didn't stop Pussy from giving a twirl as she approached him. The black of the dress spun about, revealing a flash of red fabric used to line the skirt. The lace shoulders were wide and striking. The lace panel in the front plunged to an almost scandalous level. It cost a pretty penny, but it was money well spent in her mind.

"Thank you, George." She padded up to him. "It is a lovely dress."

"Sure," he smiled, "but I wasn't talking about the dress."

She felt a flush run through her cheeks. "Well, Mr. Pup, you can certainly cut a nice figure yourself. It's nice to see you in something other than a fireman's uniform."

"The invitation said formal dress," he looked down at himself, "so I had to dig out my old tux. Does it still fit okay?"

Her eyes scanned up and down in an instant. "Most definitely." A couple of steps closer let her wrap her arms around him and pull him into a hug. "It's good to see you, George. Thank you for meeting me."

"It's good to see you, too, Pussy. I've been worried." He distanced himself just enough to allow him to extend his arm towards her.

Her right hand slipped in through the crook in his elbow and she took the first step towards the front door of the hotel. "I'm fine, George, but thank you. It's always nice to have someone who cares that much."

He took a deep breath as he reached for the door. "Are you sure this is going to work?"

"Not at all," Pussy smiled, "but that's never stopped me before."

The door opened and they stepped into the grand lobby of the Velvet Arms. The cacophonous din of conversation and laughter hit them like a cold slap. It was a hollow sound, created by the incessant ramblings of people working to impress themselves.

The exact type of crowd that Pussy expected Drago to enjoy.

"What now?" George asked.

"We mingle." Pussy pulled on his arm, angling towards a small gathering. Four men and two women gathered in a semi-circle. From the way they stood together, the two men who arrived with the women were more than a little concerned about leaving under the same arrangement.

"…continues to be a menace to our yard." The man held his hand to his lapel, as if supporting his own ego by physical strength.

"Hello," Pussy wasted no time as she approached. "I am so very sorry to interrupt. I'm not disturbing you, am I?"

The men looked at Pussy in the way the other women were hoping they would look at them. The women, in turn, looked at Pussy in the exact opposite manner.

"Not at all, Miss…?" One of the apparently unoccupied men asked.

"Kathman. Patricia Kathman." She pulled herself a little closer to the man on her arm. "And this is George. Isn't he delightful?"

"A pleasure to meet you both," one of the other men stated. "How can we help you?"

"We're here for Mr. Drago's gathering, and I'm rather embarrassed to admit that I'm not sure where to go. The invitation wasn't clear." She twirled her finger in a loose circle while staring into the man's eyes.

"I think I can assist you with that." The closer man stepped between them and leaned in towards Pussy. "If you look over there you can see those men beside that door." She let go of George's arm and pressed against the other man's body. Her head almost lay on top of his shoulder as she looked down the length of his arm.

"Oh, yes!" she giggled.

She heard him swallow. "Well, that's where you want to go. They'll handle everything for you."

"Oh, thank you so much, Mr…?"

"Foster. Carl Foster." He took hold of her hand and brought it up to almost touch his nose. "I hope to see you upstairs."

"One never knows…." She took the extra moment to wink at him before returning to George's arm. "Come along, George, we don't want to disturb these nice people any longer." She looked over at them. "Thank you all again."

Six steps later she glanced over her shoulder. Three of the men were still staring at her. One of the women still held her in an icy gaze as well. The other man and woman were in a hushed, but seemingly heated discussion.

"Isn't he delightful?" George repeated in an bewildered tone.

"It set the stage and kept the focus away from you," Pussy answered. "Besides, you are delightful."

There was a gruff, barely audible cough from him.

"By the way, here." Pussy held up an envelope. Fine linen paper with a gold wax seal. George took it in his hand.

"What is this?"

"We had to get an invitation somehow." She smiled. "And I don't think that this party is going to miss that gentleman at all."

"You stole this?" George forced out the whisper. "Does Fizz let you do that, too?"

"No," Pussy answered, "but years of living with Coney did." She didn't mean to say her name. She had to force her hand to relax on George's arm. "And if they're checking names, you're Carl Foster, and I'm your plus one."

As they walked, Pussy noticed the silence and looked over at George. He kept glancing at her sideways.

"What?" she asked.

"I'm not sure I like this side of you," he chuckled.

"Don't worry." She moved in closer to him. "It only comes out when needed."

The two men beside the door leading to Drago's private elevator were new to Pussy. From their size and demeanor, these were employees and not bodyguards.

"Good evening." The one who spoke smiled with too many teeth and an odd accent. "May I see your invitation please?"

George handed it over with two fingers.

The man took it and pulled the inner invite free. As he looked at it, Pussy smiled at the other man. Like his companion, he had pale fur and dark eyes. His face was long and thin, and he seemed slightly frightened. Desiree mentioned there were men on that same floor with her.

"Welcome to the party, sir. I hope you and your companion have a lovely evening." The man opened up the door and stepped to one side. "Press the top button and it will take you to Mr. Drago's residence."

George gestured for Pussy to enter and then followed her inside. There was already a key in the panel, and only two of the buttons were lit up. The lobby and the eighteenth floor. She waited for George to push the button.

"That went smoother than I expected," George said.

"It's not done yet," Pussy countered. "I just hope Detective Ringtail is able to follow through with her part."

"Don't worry about Lila," George answered. "She'll get it done."

Pussy turned her head to him and raised an eyebrow. "Lila?"

"Yes. A rather impressive woman. She'll be able to handle it, I promise." He smiled, but she wasn't entirely sure it was at her.

"I'm wondering if that's all she's been handling." Pussy hated saying the words the moment they left her mouth.

"What's that supposed to mean?" George pulled his head back slightly.

"We don't have time for this conversation right now, George." Her voice went soft and she took hold of his arm again. "But I promise you we will have it."

"Did I do something?" He asked. "You're talking like I did something."

"Later, George. We have work to do." Pussy let go of his arm. "Speaking of which…."

Her hand went down the front of her dress and returned with a small vial of red liquid.

"Is that what I think it is?" George asked.

"It is. And I think it's best that I take it now before we arrive." She popped the cork loose.

"Are you sure? How long does it last?"

"Normally about an hour, but that can vary depending on how much I exert myself." She held it up. "Don't worry. I have another one, just in case."

"Is there anything I need to do?" He eyed the vial.

"If I start to fall, catch me. Otherwise, I should be fine." She lifted it up to her mouth. "Bottoms up."

She felt herself falling. The world was streaming up past her in a rush of color and motion. Details were lost in the blur. At least until she held her hand out. She stopped. A dragon's tail broke, replaced by a sword. She started to fall again. Her hand went out. A long splinter of wood piercing through the palm of her hand and traveled through the top and out. She fell again. Her hand went out. A silver chain fell to the ground and turned black.

"Pussy?" George's voice was distant, but getting closer. "Pussy are you all right?"

She blinked. Her head was against George's chest. He had his hands wrapped around her, holding her up.

Brushing herself off, she stood back up. "How long was I out?"

"A second. Maybe two." He took a deep breath. "Is it always like that?"

"Not at all. It's different each and every time," she mumbled.

The elevator chimed and came to a stop. She looped her arm back around his just as the door slid to the side and revealed the room beyond.

Everything remained as she remembered. An arched ceiling above her with a blue sky mural. Two mock-gold statues of alligator women holding swords. The only new addition was a beautiful young woman waiting just outside the elevator.

"Welcome," she gestured to her left, "the party is through there. Enjoy your evening."

"Thank you," George answered. They hadn't made it out of the entry before he spoke again. "This place is really nice."

Pussy almost stopped in mid stride. Instead, she just looked over at him. "Remind me to have a conversation with you regarding style, taste, and restraint when this is over."

"What? I like it."

"I repeat my previous statement."

He didn't have time to argue any further. They moved out into the massive holding room. Already it was almost full of people. Easily fifty if not more.

"I'm not sure this is within fire code," George mumbled.

Pussy laughed. "I'll keep that in mind." She pulled him into the room and the gathered crowd.

"So, who exactly are we looking for?" He did his best to stay by her side, but fell back a time or two.

"I'm looking for the bartender at the moment. I have a feeling I know who it will be." She maneuvered them towards the center of the room. "Besides, I think we both could use a drink."

"Won't that mess up the Fizz?" His voice went to a whisper at the end of the sentence.

"No. I'm fine in that regard. Wait just a second." Her lungs filled up and Pussy let the party happen around her. Individual sounds came to her and she began to sort through them. One by one she placed them into categories and slid them aside, searching out a particular sound. Ice hitting glass. A woman's accented voice.

"This way." Pussy wrapped her arm around George's and led him through the crowd. Most people moved out of the way, but the few who didn't were easy enough to navigate past.

They broke through the mass of people to see a couple standing with their backs to them at the bar. Before Pussy could say a word the couple walked off, revealing a familiar face.

"George, I would like to introduce you to Desiree." Pussy let go of George's arm as they arrived at the bar. "I have to say that she is a most remarkable bartender."

"Miss…you came." Her head darted back and forth, scanning the crowd.

"I told you I would. You're going to leave here with me tonight." Pussy leaned into the bar. "I promise."

"How? There are all these people. And Mr. Drago, he…he won't let me go."

"Leave that to me." Pussy raised her head. "In the meantime, I'm going to take advantage of your knowledge. Would you recommend another whiskey for me?"

"Of course, ma'am." She turned to grab a bottle.

"How are you getting her out of here?" George whispered.

"Through the door, of course," Pussy stated.

"Here you are, ma'am. Mr. Drago allowed for a more complete bar this evening. I believe you will find this very satisfying." She placed the glass on the bar, giving it a slight turn as she pushed it towards Pussy.

The aroma hit Pussy's nose well before the glass reached her mouth. A strong oak preceded the taste. Pussy pulled out smokey, malty flavors that ended with an austere finish. "Wow." She pulled the glass back. "I'm going to have to drink Fizz before whiskey more often."

"Ma'am?" Desiree twisted her head.

"What would you like, George?" Pussy moved to a new subject.

"Hmm?" His head turned towards them. "I'm sorry. I was looking through the room. Seeing if…I knew anyone."

"Give it a few more minutes. In the meantime, I want you to trust Desiree. She has an amazing sense of taste. Tell her what you like, and she'll surprise you." She looked back at the exotic bartender. "Do you know where Mr. Drago is right now?"

"Attention!" A loud voice rose above the crowd noise. "Everyone, thank you. Thank you for coming."

"Never mind. I seem to have found him." Pussy took a half step away from George.

"As you know, I wanted everyone to be here to meet a special guest." Drago stood beside a short, dry, weathered looking rat of a man. Behind both of them stood Neko Mata and Tayra. "This is Ker Musho. He is an honored guest visiting us from overseas."

A polite applause rose up.

"You have Mr. Musho to thank for this lovely evening. Please, let's do our best to make him feel welcome. Enjoy the occasion, and thank you again for coming." A second polite applause ended his speech.

"George, I want you to stay here." Pussy picked up her glass. "If something bad happens, do your best to make sure everyone here gets out safely."

"Pussy, this isn't part of the plan." George stepped towards her.

"Actually, it is. Detective Ringtail and I just didn't want you to get upset." She touched him lightly on the cheek. "Don't worry. I've been in worse scrapes than this."

"You're not in one yet. It could get—"

"Work with the crowd. Help Detective Ringtail finish this. I'll be fine." She turned to Desiree. "Trust George like you would me. He'll help you out."

"Yes, ma'am." Desiree replied.

She stepped away and walked into the crowd. It was much easier to weave her way through the throng of conversing socialites without George beside her. Even if she did have to ignore the men trying their best to get her attention.

They hadn't gotten far. Drago and his guest of honor were speaking to a group of two couples. Her gait slowed and her hips swayed as she walked up to join them.

"…quite a journey." The group laughed.

"Yes, but it will be worth it." Mr. Musho's accent was harsh and sharp. "I am hoping that the dealings in business with Mr. Drago will benefit us both greatly."

"He doesn't have it." Pussy felt the group's eyes shift towards her. Her gaze fixated on Mr. Musho. "It seems that Mr. Drago misplaced what he promised you a few days ago."

"What?" He turned to look at Drago. "Is this true?"

Pussy looked over to see Drago's lip twitch slightly. The two bodyguards behind him flinched, but Drago held them in place with a hand motion. "I have to commend your audacity." He looked down to her feet and back to her face. "As well as your beauty."

"You flatter me, Drago." She turned her head slightly. "It appears you didn't have a chance to talk to your honored guest about the little accident that lost your shipment."

"Drago, what is she talking about? Who is this woman?" Mr. Musho stomped a tiny foot against the floor.

"Oh, I'm sorry. Where are my manners?" Drago opened his palm towards her. "May I present to everyone Miss Pussy Katnip. She's making a bit of a name for herself lately."

"I try," she replied.

"Oh, and Miss Katnip," Drago stepped over to one of the couples, "may I present to you Captain Saunders of the Mutt Town Police Department." He looked at the Captain with a raised eyebrow. "I do believe you've been looking for her."

The Captain stepped out. He was a tall and thin, but far from fragile. "Pussy Katnip, you're under arrest for the murder of Coney Hase."

A snort of a laugh came from her right. She was pretty sure it was Tayra, but she really didn't care.

Her mouth curled up into a half smile. A fang flashed in the front of her teeth.

Chapter Nineteen

"Why am I here again?"

"Because I adore your company," Lila answered.

"I'm serious, Ringtail," Stye grumbled. "I could be doin' a dozen other things that actually sound productive. I hate bein' some goon with a badge."

"Look, there is a good chance that something bad is going to happen. Maybe to me, maybe by me. In either case, I'm probably gonna need backup. You still willing to think of me as a cop?"

"You still got a badge, don't ya?" He nodded.

"Yeah, well, the day's not over yet," she mumbled. "Wait, I think this is it."

Pussy described the door as looking like any other, except for the handle. Only when she exited down the stairs from the seventeenth floor did she notice the difference. The outside handle looked like the others in the hallway at a glance, but there wasn't a functional keyhole.

"Yeah, this is it." Lila stood in front of the door and pulled out her deck of cigarettes. She took one right from the pack and brought the other hand up with a match that lit along the way.

Stye went to the handle. It didn't budge. "Okay, well…. Hey, there's no keyhole."

"That's the one." Lila put her cigarettes back in her right pocket. When her hand came back out, it held something else. "Watch the hallway, would you?"

Lila knelt down in front of the door.

"What are you doin'?" Stye asked.

"Breaking in." Her lips held the cigarette in limbo. It wasn't firmly in her mouth, but somehow it didn't fall. "Old skills."

"You can't do that!" Stye put his hand on her shoulder and pushed. She didn't move. "That's against the law. We're cops!"

"Y'know, I can honestly say that you do impress me sometimes. Not sure that's a good thing yet." She shrugged and his hand fell off her shoulder. "Just keep your eyes open."

"I don't like this," he griped.

"You don't have to." Lila worked the apparatus into the gap between the door and the jamb. It resembled the hybrid offspring of a screwdriver and a spatula.

"What is that?" Stye asked.

"Don't know what they call them around here…" The words weren't able to form with her mouth hanging open. "…when I was back on the streets in Motor City we called it…" She felt the click in her hand as clearly as she heard it. "…a slip knife."

The motion of the door pushed the smell of stale air out of the stairwell.

"And why do you have one?" Stye's voice went up as he spoke.

A long thread of smoke climbed from her mouth. "Because I used to be back on the streets of Motor City?" She shoved the tool back in her pocket. "Let's go."

It was a long flight of stairs. About half again what she expected. It was still just a single flight, however. Not even a whisper of sound came from the hinges as she swung the exit open.

"Okay," she pointed down the hall, "it's supposed to be down that way. You stay here. If you see anyone coming, get me. Got it?"

"Any problem and I talk to you. Yeah, yeah. I got it." Stye waved his hand once.

"And Stye," she waited until he looked at her, "thanks."

He stood there just staring. She could almost see the wheels turning inside his head. "Yeah, well, just hurry. I still hate this."

It was a short walk to the end of the hallway. The slight alcoves containing doors all seemed the same. At least until she got to the end. A set of double doors stood out from the others and called her over. She pulled the cigarette from her mouth with her left hand. The thumb and forefinger from her right crushed the fire out. The half-used butt went into her jacket pocket. The badge came out of her lapel pocket.

She held the badge up at shoulder level as she knocked on the door.

He was buttoning his cufflinks. The tie around his neck was somewhere between resting on his neck and being properly tied. Despite his somewhat disheveled look, the man cut a smart figure. A square face with deep set dark eyes. His eyes danced from her badge to her face.

"Can I help you?" he asked.

"Detective Ringtail, MTPD." She slipped the badge back into it's home pocket. "Are you Julian Perro?"

"Yes." The hesitation in his voice was growing.

"I'd like to come in and speak with you, Mr. Perro." She pointed past him.

"Now's not a good time," he answered. "And how did you get up here?" He stuck his head out enough to glance down the hall.

"Like I said, MTPD." She moved closer to the door. "Is it true that you are the accountant for Mr. Conner Drago?"

"I'm actually his financial coordinator. It's a little more complicated." His eyes narrowed. "What is this in regards to, Detective?"

"Following up on a couple of leads." Her foot slid forward. "I'd appreciate some time to speak with you inside."

"If you would like to leave a card, I'll come see you tomorrow. Tonight, I have other plans. I'm sorry." He pushed the door half closed, intent on shutting her out.

Her body banged against it as she pushed inside. He recoiled back into his room. "Sorry, but I insist." Lila pushed past him and into his apartment. "Lovely place."

"I'm going to ask you to leave, Detective! This instant!" He loomed above her with his left arm pointed towards the door.

"Tell me, Mr. Perro, do you keep all records here on the premises?" Two doors and one short hallway were the other ways out of the room. The three windows were another way, but not one she wanted to explore.

"I'm not going to tell you a third time, Detective. Leave. Now." A rumble grew behind his voice.

"Sure," she nodded. "Before I do, though, can you show me all your files regarding Mr. Drago's finances?"

"Come back with a warrant, Detective." He stepped around her, putting her between him and the door. "I'm going to escort you from my apartment now."

Lila turned towards him. "Why are you so unwilling to answer my questions? Are you hiding something Mr. Perro?"

"I don't want to call security, Detective, but—"

"That's a good plan. Why don't you call your security, and I'll call mine? We can have everyone meet here for a nice long talk." She watched his eyes. They shifted.

"Why are you here alone, Detective? Shouldn't you have someone else with you?" His stance widened. "Can I see your badge again?"

Lila smiled. "I don't want to take up too much of your time, Mr. Perro." She stepped backwards. "I'll come back tomorrow, if that works better."

He moved forward. She retreated with each step. "Make sure you bring that warrant, Detective. I don't like someone harassing me in my own home."

"No one does, Mr. Perro." She turned to the door and opened it up. After stepping out, she turned back towards him. "Oh, and one other thing. Thank you for your time." She extended her hand towards him.

He looked down at it and then back at her face. "Good night, Detective."

The door closed on her, almost hitting her nose. Her hand slipped inside her pocket as she turned. The cigarette moved right back to her mouth. "I thought as much."

She pulled out matches and lit the remaining stub. Each step away from the door was more casual than the one before it. She wasn't planning on walking far.

Two alcoves down, she found her destination. Not too far out of the hallway, but it was enough to give her some space. Then, the waiting began.

As she suspected, it didn't take long. She heard the door shut down the corridor. His footsteps carried the dull sound of shoes on carpet, but had a tempo with a purpose.

He walked past the alcove without even a glance her direction. The only change she made after he passed was to move to the other side of the alcove, away from any glance back.

The chime of the elevator rung through the hallway. The grind of the rollers as the doors opened and then closed again was the last thing she needed to hear.

A glance to confirm no one was in the hall with her, and she moved back to Julian Perro's door. She pulled the slip knife from her pocket. It took less than six seconds for her to hear the click of the latch springing open.

The door closed with a slight click behind her.

Wasting no time, she moved towards the hallway leading off the main room. Two bedrooms waited for her. She glanced inside the first one and found exactly what she wanted.

The desk was oak, and filled a full quarter of the room. The wood wainscoting matched the finish and the construction of the furniture itself. The carvings on the edges of the desk were enough to make it look expensive, but not enough to push it over to pretentious. The chair behind it was simple and practical, and not close to a match for the desk itself. The top of the desk was neat and organized, and as clean as a baby's bottom.

There were five drawers on the desk. Two on either side and a large central one. A tug on the central one went nowhere. The lock on the drawer was the one that came with the desk. The same slip knife opened it up in just two seconds.

Pencils. Pens. Paperclips. Everything that a desk would have and a few extras that seemed appropriate for a book keeper. Nothing she cared about at all.

With the central one opened, the side drawers came free. Nothing. Nothing. Nothing. And finally, nothing. Plenty of notes and files, but not what she hoped—what she wanted—to see.

The chair squeaked when she sat down. She stared across the room and heard her teeth grind inside her head. Then they stopped. She looked at the door to the room, and then back at the wall.

She popped up and walked to stand beside the door. Her eye ran from the top of the wall down to the base.

"That's not straight," she muttered.

Her hand caressed the wall as she stepped towards the corner of the room. It slipped down onto the wainscoting and pressed. It bowed under the pressure of her hand. Like a present on her birthday, it opened up to reveal a surprise.

Two shallow shelves held standing accordion folders. She pulled them both out and looked at the contents. The line of her mouth turned into a curve. "Bingo."

"I have to admit, I was hoping I was wrong." His voice made her jump. The folders fell to the ground, spilling a few pages. "But here you are."

Julian Perro stood in the doorway shaking his head.

"You're pretty quiet when you want to be," Lila commented. "And I'm a little surprised, myself. I didn't think you saw me."

"I didn't. But there was an odd smell that I passed in the hallway. I was already at Mr. Drago's penthouse before I recognized it. Cigarettes are a nasty habit, my dear." He slipped his jacket from his shoulders.

"I'm surprised you came back by yourself." Lila stood up and took a step away from the wall.

"I didn't want to disturb anyone else. This was my problem, after all." He folded his jacket and laid it on the floor.

Lila pointed to the folders. "Katnip was right. You do keep records of everything. There's enough in that to put Drago— and you, by the way—behind bars for a very long time."

"Oh, you know Miss Katnip? I don't know why I am genuinely surprised by that." He loosened his tie. "What a shame. She is such a lovely woman."

She shook her head and moved behind the desk. "I don't suppose it's going to help if I say that you're under arrest."

He removed his cuff links and rolled up his sleeves. "No, I'm sorry my dear. It will not."

"I'm a cop," she informed him.

"And I came home to find an intruder. Simple self defense." His hands came up in front of his body.

"Fair enough," she replied.

He moved faster than she expected. It took her a second to realize that he had punched her in the face. She saw the second one coming through a haze of confusion, but was too slow to avoid it.

Before a third one could land she pushed the chair at him and scrambled backwards. "What the heck?"

"I was EUBC champion in my country when I was nineteen." He danced towards her. "I gave it up when I realized how little future there was in it."

"Good for you." She jumped away and began to circle back around the desk. "I knocked a kid's tooth out on the playground when I was thirteen. By accident, but still…."

"What a shame. I was hoping you might know how to fight." He lunged at her.

"Never said I didn't. I just don't know anything about boxing." His jaw shifted as her fist collided with it. He staggered back. "I know how to fight dirty."

She lunged at him. From what she could tell, her knee going into his stomach seemed to hurt. And he really didn't like it when she drove her heel onto the top of his foot.

Something pulled her hair loose out of its bun. By the time she figured out that Julian was filling his fist with her locks, her head was already connecting with the wall. And it did three more times.

As she collapsed to the floor, he stepped away.

She blinked a couple of times and saw him wiping the top of his loafers with a handkerchief. "Look what you did to my shoes! These cost seventy-five dollars!"

"Bill me." The groaned words were the last thing out of her mouth before her teeth sank into his calf.

He screamed, shook his leg, and punched down at her. She let him go before the punch landed. He stood directly above her. It seemed like a great opportunity to drive her foot up between his legs.

The sound he issued wasn't exactly a scream, but it was certainly one of distress. Lila rolled up to a standing position, and repaid his kindness by grabbing him by his conveniently loosened necktie.

Lila jumped onto the desk, dragging his head by the neck. Julian's body arched backwards against the press of her feet against his lower back. Both hands held tightly to the necktie and pulled. The sharp slap of his hands against the desktop was as close as he came to touching her. After a minute or so, those stopped. She didn't.

Her hand started to cramp, so she let go. Julian Perro slipped from the desk and fell to the floor on the other side.

"I knew I should'a brought that nightstick." Lila's voice was weak, but steady. A long pace around the desk gave her the reassurance she wanted. He was still on the floor, unmoving.

The cop took over and she moved to touch his neck. A heartbeat thrummed against her fingers. She pulled a pair of cuffs from her back pocket and secured his arms behind his back. She rifled through his pockets, pulling out their contents. The one thing she wanted went into a pocket of her own. Everything else stayed on his desk.

All of her attention turned to the folders and the scattered pages on the floor. The papers crunched as she forced them back inside. A few wrinkles wouldn't hurt their value.

When she stood back up, her head didn't stop with the rest of her body. The room swelled and twisted around her long enough to give her pause, but not long enough to stop her.

Her feet didn't agree with her idea of walking briskly through the apartment and into the hall, either. At least not at first. Every step pushed her, and she pushed right back. By the time she reached the emergency stairwell she was ready for a cigarette.

"Stye!" She pulled the butt from the pack with her lips. He opened the door just as she got it lit.

"Holy snot! What happened to you?" His head moved like a cheap bobblehead doll. "You're bleedin' like a stuck pig!"

She ignored the obvious joke. "I am?" Her fingers came back from her forehead with dark red highlights. "Aw, great. Just what I need."

"You don't look so good," Stye proclaimed.

"Yeah, well, you should see the other guy." Her thumb jerked back over her shoulder. "In fact, go do that. I've got him cuffed up. Last door on the right."

"You might wanna see a croaker about that head." He pointed as though she didn't know the location.

"I'll do that." She tapped the folder in her hand. "But I've got some paperwork I need to share first."

"What is that?" he asked.

"A special surprise for the host of the shindig upstairs. I'm gonna go show it to him." She took a step towards the elevator.

"You know you gotta have a key to get in there, right?" Stye said.

The jangling sound of metal on metal accompanied her raising her hand. "Yep. I took the liberty of borrowing one from our handcuffed friend."

"That Drago guy ain't gonna be too happy to see you showin' him those files, y'know." Stye shook his head. "Sure you don't want me going with you?"

The door chimed and opened beside her. "Nah, that's okay. I've got some folks waiting for me already." She stepped into the elevator car. "It's gonna be a real party."

The door closed and carried her up one flight.

Chapter Twenty

"No, I don't think so."

There must have been something in what she said. Or in the way that she said it. Because everyone stared at her with the exact same expression.

"I beg your pardon?" It was Captain Saunders who was the first to answer.

"I have a great deal of respect for your position, Captain. And I assure you that when this plays out, I will turn myself over to Detective Ringtail." Pussy took enough time for a breath. "But not right now. First, we need to deal with the elephant in the room. Or, more precisely, the dragon."

"I don't think that insulting Mr. Drago is going to help your case, Miss Katnip," Saunders said.

The din of the room had decreased. Pussy let that sink in for everyone around her.

"This is ridiculous." The rasp in Drago's voice threatened to become a snarl. "Take her into custody, Captain. Or do I need to show you how to do that?"

"Why don't I take you all into custody instead?"

Pussy turned to her left. The blood coating the arriving woman's face only added to the drama. "Welcome, Detective. I was worried you might not make it."

"Oh, I wouldn't miss this party," she answered. "Captain, Conner Drago has been actively participating in acts of international slavery for over two years. I have evidence right here."

The crowd had died down to a low murmur by the time she spoke.

"That's ridiculous!" Drago blurted out. "I've done no such thing!"

"Depends on how you look at it." Pussy turned to him. "You take young men and women and exploit them. Find a weakness and put them under your thumb. Create a situation where they have no freedom or any hope of ever leaving."

"And it isn't illegal. I think you might want to reconsider your accusations, Miss Katnip." Drago threw his arms in the air. "And I don't know why we're having this conversation anyway. You are a wanted felon. I am an innocent man being persecuted in his own home."

"I wouldn't go that far." Detective Ringtail passed through a line of her own cigarette smoke. "What she's describing is called indentured servitude. It's been illegal for almost a hundred years now." She took another drag. "Oh, and it is considered slavery, by the way."

A rumble grew in Drago's throat. "I don't know what you think you've found, but there isn't enough in any of those files."

"You're financial expert kept some pretty good records." Detective Ringtail tapped on the folder once more. "Lot's of details."

"And, I do believe you just admitted to it in front of," Pussy glanced around, "close to a hundred witnesses, I'd guess." Her eyes became slits. "You're going to pay for what you did to Coney."

"I told you," he growled, "I didn't kill her."

"I know," Pussy snarled back, "but you drove her to where she was and I blame you for the end result."

A shadow rose up behind him. The silence of the crowd broke into a cacophony of screams. Like a nightmare forced into the real world, the dragon woke.

Chaos spiraled away from the pale draconic form. People trampled over themselves, rushing towards the elevator. A few ran down hallways, ignoring everything but their desire to flee.

Only two people stood their ground.

"Tayra, get that file." Drago pointed at Detective Ringtail. "Neko," Pussy's eyes locked with the dragon's as he stepped forward, "kill Miss Katnip."

Chapter Twenty-One

It was just a blur in front of her. She saw something white move, taking Pussy Katnip with it. Her head turned to see the dragon rushing across the room with Pussy held tight.

"Stupid dame." The clever repartee was the only warning she got. Drago's thug wasn't the dapper figure of Julian Perro, but he was certainly a man who was hard to ignore. His hand extended towards her like the claw of a crane. "Ya shouldn'ta brought those files up here."

He was big, but he was also slow. Lila jumped backwards and his hand swiped at so much empty air. Chaos still surrounded them. Screams of panic and people rushing around were everywhere. She didn't want to make it worse.

"Right now all you're guilty of is being a thug. Don't do anything stupid, and you might even be able to walk out of here." It was worth a try, even if she knew the ultimate result.

He didn't say anything. Once more his hand reached out to grab her, and again she stepped away. From the corner of her eye she saw Drago heading towards the hallway.

"Okay, have it your way." The folder was in her left hand. Her right hand drove into the big man's midsection. There was a sharp cry of pain.

From her, not from him.

"You don't punch like the Katnip broad." His hand passed just above her head as she ducked down. "Besides, I put on some extra protection to be safe."

Lila flexed her hand open and closed a couple of times. "What is it, a steel plate?"

"Uh-huh," he replied.

She danced backwards as he plodded towards her. "Then I guess I won't be punching you there again."

"I don't care. I gotta get that folder. You give it to me, and I'll only hurt you a bit." His feet hit the floor like twin hams on the end of posts.

"Why don't we consider this a draw. That way we both walk out of here intact." She looked right. Two couches and a long coffee table. The only thing to her left were people rushing the exit.

"Nope. Gimme the folder." He reached out still missing by inches. Something had to be around to help her. She turned her back to him just for a moment.

That's when George ran past her.

She heard the impact before she saw it. George was on Tayra, pummeling him repeatedly.

"I've got this!" George yelled. "Go after Drago!"

"That guy is huge! I don't want—"

"Lila!" The time he looked at her was inconsequential. The eye contact was anything but. "Go. Get him."

She sprinted towards the hallway. A multitude of voices came from the far end of it. They joined together to create an indistinct sound that she could only describe as panicked.

"Not there," she murmured. "He wouldn't go into a panicky mob."

She turned in place. The contents of the hall passed in front of her like a slow carousel. The hallway down. A wall with four paintings—three odd abstract monstrosities and one over-worked portrait of Drago himself. The hallway back. The other wall with two wall sconces and a full-length mirror sporting a border so ornate it threatened to begin crawling on its own power. And then back to the hallway down.

The images repeated in her mind. She turned back to the mirror. Her own reflection stood before her, but didn't meet her gaze. She was looking just to the right.

Lila stepped to the mirror. Lifting the hem of her jacket gave her enough room to stuff the folder down the back of her pants. It also freed up both of her hands.

The intricate edges of the frame passed under her fingers. She moved along them with delicate care. Searching for something unseen.

A click. The mirror moved.

The only sound was the faint scrape of the frame against the carpet as it swung open. A narrow hallway waited. Lila entered. She wasn't sure how far she had gone when the mirror closed back up. Lights shined ahead of her, providing a beacon for direction.

The red tint spilled into the hallway like blood turned ablaze. A deep red covered everything inside the room. Walls. Floor. Every table covering. The items on the tables were a variety of colors. The man standing in the middle was dark green.

"This is my trophy room." Drago looked around him at the contents. "I've collected so many different things from my travels. My favorites I've put in here."

"I'll make sure they're carefully catalogued." Lila stepped into the room. "You're under arrest."

"You know, Detective, I hoped that you would simply let go of everything. Allow the case to take the path towards the best conclusion." Drago meandered about, not once looking her way.

"I suppose that means arresting Pussy Katnip in your mind." Lila paced after him.

"Of course. She made herself the perfect target. Witnesses and all. Ready for conviction." He faced her. His eyes were as red as the room around him. "But you had to be the detective, didn't you?"

"It's in my job title." With each step she closed the distance between them.

"True, but I was counting on your birthright." He raised his head up, eyes looking down past his snout. "It's why I allowed Saunders to bring you here."

She stopped. "I beg your pardon?"

"Saunders said he wanted you. Said you would fit in here. I doubted him, but then he told me about you, and I thought it was an obvious choice." His lip curled up. "A 'coon on the force? Perfect."

Everything slowed. Lila took the time to reach into her pocket. The pack of cigarettes crumpled in her hand as she pulled them free from a pocket. One of them peeked from the top. She pulled it out and flipped it around. One tap on the back of her hand and she put it into her mouth. The pack made its way back, and her hand returned with a book of matches. One flared to life and transferred it's life to the cigarette in Lila's mouth. She pulled in a long, steady breath, bringing the gasper's tip to a bright glow to match the color of the room.

"Now that's just rude." The smoke exited along with her words. "You didn't hear me calling you a handbag, did you?"

He flinched. She didn't.

"Where are my files!" he demanded.

"Doesn't matter. Turn around and put your hands on your head." Lila had to try.

"Let me show you something." There were several tables lined up to his right. He went to the first one and grasped something from it. She recognized the generals of it, if not the specifics. "This is something that I picked up in my travels to the Orient. I traded a lovely young woman to a local lord for it. He proclaimed it to be almost a sacred item."

The sword pulled free of its sheath. She expected a shine from the blade, but got a dull mottled grey instead.

"Turns out those people can make a good sword. Sharp as anything I've ever seen." As if to illustrate his point, he sliced across the top of the table. The candle on top of it fell into two clean sections. Lila took a step backwards.

"Good-bye Detective." He was rushing forward. Her eyes were on everything except him. The first piece of metal she saw went into her hand.

The sword cut through the air with a whistle, countered by the sharp clang of metal at the end. She was barely able to raise the candlestick up in time. The steel blade cut into the softer metal, leaving a nick in the surface. She pictured the sword cutting through her flesh like so much butter.

"Very good. I appreciate the effort." Drago's arms arced overhead. Lila swung her own version of a weapon high, knocking the blade to one side. Just not far enough. It caught her in the meat of her right leg. At first she wasn't sure that it broke skin. The sudden rush of blood down her leg convinced her otherwise.

He was relentless. She was lucky. Time and again he tried to remove any part of her body, but Lila kept them all. It wouldn't last, and she knew it.

Her left foot came up and landed against his thigh. It bounced off like a rubber ball. And he laughed. He had thick skin. She couldn't generate any force with one leg.

Something had to change.

She scrambled backwards. It wasn't enough distance to keep him away, and she was counting on that. The cigarette came out of her mouth and into her empty hand. Years of practice let her flick the lit butt at her target. It his just above his right eye. The ash and sparks rained down into it.

His scream died against the walls. He covered his eye and reared back his head. She wouldn't get a better chance.

The candlestick hit his throat, causing a wet, crunching sound. Now his head was down, and his hand at his neck. Even so, he towered over her.

She had to leap up so that she could bring the candlestick down onto the top of his head. After the second shot he fell to his knees. Three more took him all the way to the ground.

The cuffs were around his wrists before she even thought to check on his health. He was alive. She took the liberty to borrow the tie from around his neck. It wrapped around her leg and did the best she could to slow the bleeding.

Hobbling her way back, the sound of chaos was considerably less noticeable. The sight of George was welcome. Especially considering that he was conscious. The bruises on his face were already swelling up. And there was more than a little bit of blood on his head.

Tayra was unconscious next to him.

"Good job." Lila announced her return.

"Lila!" George rose to his feet and limped over to her. "You're hurt!"

There was no chance of her holding back the laugh. "Have you looked in a mirror?"

"I've already called an ambulance. They should be here any minute." His hands went to her thigh. "Let me look at that. Sit down."

"I'm okay with that plan." She made her way to the couch and sat down with a grimace. He started pulling her pants leg open.

"That's pretty deep." He looked up into her eyes. "How are you feeling?"

"Right now, pretty good." She looked down at him holding her thigh.

"Detective Ringtail." She wasn't expecting that voice. "Tell me what's going on."

"Captain Saunders." Her eyes redirected to the man walking towards them. "I expected you to be gone by now."

"People needed help," he answered. "Where's Drago?"

Her thumb motioned over her right shoulder. "Secret room. He's gonna need an ambulance, too."

"Are you all right?" He stood over them. George was still working with her wound.

"I'll live." Her hand snaked around behind her. "Oh, and you might be interested to know that this paperwork also has a rather extensive list of police officers who accepted money from him."

His eyes glazed. "I can explain."

"No, you can't. You can offer excuses, but you can't explain it." She shook her head. "You don't get that luxury right now."

He stood in silence for a minute. "I think I wanted you to find out. That's why I brought you down here. You're the best detective I've ever known."

"Well, good thing I did it, then, huh?" She winced. George was doing something unpleasant. "I'm a little occupied right now, Captain. I'm willing to bet that you can find someone downstairs who will be more than happy to take you in."

His mouth opened. Her look shut it. He turned to walk away.

"And Captain," Lila got his attention, "don't make me come find you."

He shuffled away without another word. Or even so much as a look back.

"I'm sorry," George whispered. "I know how much he meant to you."

The way he was looking at her, she didn't notice the pain in her leg. "That's okay. It was time for me to find new people to care about."

George stood up. She could hear the sound of medics rushing into the room. Her eyes went to them, and then looked around at the destruction. One question leapt to her mind.

"Where's Pussy Katnip?"

Chapter Twenty-Two

The beast hit her like a train. There were screams around her, but the loudest sound in her ears was her breathing. It was already rough and ragged. The dragon—Neko Mata—had cracked some ribs at the very least.

A sharper sound announced itself. The pain shooting through her back provided the explanation. The broken pieces of bar that appeared around her gave the location.

He roared. She smelled the brimstone stench of his breath and the heat that came with it. For a moment she wondered if he would be foolish enough to actually let loose a gout of fire inside the building.

That's when the claw raked across her shoulder. He had reached around behind her, perhaps with the intent of grabbing hold again. All he was able to manage was a brief grip, which she turned free. Not without a cost. Four gashes opened up on her left.

Her fist sank into his side. Once. Twice. Three times she drove it home. Each time it seemed to sink a little deeper into him. It was enough to get him to release her.

Pussy sprung to her feet. Neko Mata crouched, turning his injured side away. He held his left arm close to his body.

"Does the arm still hurt?" she prodded. "I seem to remember hearing a crack. Did I break it?"

He roared again. A little louder this time.

This time she was ready. He was faster than she remembered. Either that or she had slowed since their first conflict. She didn't want to consider that option.

She met him force for force. His momentum powered into her punch. His body twisted from the impact. As his arm came around, Pussy moved. It passed over her head, pulling a few hairs loose.

His tail was another matter. Her legs swept out from under her, sending her airborne as it sliced beneath her. The logical continuation was that she should follow that with hitting the ground. When it didn't happen she was surprised.

Neko Mata grabbed her by one arm and one leg. His entire body twisted around in a full circle before releasing her.

The window shattered around her. Unlike her last trip through panes of glass, this one left no deep cuts behind. She tumbled across the patio, crashing into the oversized table and coming to a sudden stop.

Through the haze clouding her mind, she could see a massive white figure looming above her. Two blinks brought him into focus. Her eyes fixed on the massive right claw poised above her chest.

"No!" Pussy didn't scream. The voice belonged to someone with an accent. A bottle crashed into the side of his face. She was showered in more glass and a dousing of undetermined liquid. At least, not until she smelled the quality whiskey.

Neko Mata's arm swung backwards. Pussy saw Desiree fly back several feet and land awkwardly.

Pussy's hand reached up to grab the table, and used that leverage to thrust her legs up. Both struck his midsection, and drove him staggering backwards.

She landed on her feet as he regained his.

"How dare you," she growled at him. "A sense of taste like her's? That woman is an artist."

It was undetermined if Neko Mata was actually capable of speaking. He followed his hissing reply with a sharp, deep inhalation. Pussy jumped away. The flame from his mouth chased after her.

She could smell burning cloth, and worse, burning hair. Smoke rose up from her side. Her hands quickly stifled the flames.

Just in time for a second gout of fire.

Her flesh seared. Blisters rose instantly. And despite her best effort, she screamed. She rolled on the floor, extinguishing the flames but not dimming the pain. Claws dug into her leg. He dragged her around in a great circle, building enough momentum to throw her into the solid stone wall.

Pussy pushed herself up. She paused on her knees to see the dragon-man standing a few feet away. His arms went wide as he took in another deep breath.

"Not again!" The fire erupted around her. With a great leap she passed through it and on beyond Neko Mata.

The table was fifteen feet of solid wood. Her hands grasped either side of it and her body twisted. Every muscle strained. The table came up off the floor and smashed against her foe.

His body crashed into the same stone wall she recently met. And something followed right behind. The wood cracked and splintered around him.

He roared in pain. She pulled the table back and swung at him again. This time it broke in half, and he fell to the floor.

Pussy sank to one knee. Burns and blood loss were taking their toll, and she knew it. Her hand fumbled into the top of her dress. It returned with a small red vial. She popped the cork and dumped the contents down her throat.

Blood. Blood and fire surrounded her. Washed away by the lap of water from the lake. Two figures emerged from the fire. She recognized George immediately. It took her a moment to make out Detective Ringtail. They both smiled at her. A kind, gentle smile. Their eyes wandered, falling onto each other. The flames behind them burned brighter, turning them into hazy silhouettes standing together. And their forms grew closer. Touching. And finally melding together. Becoming one. As they…kissed?

The roar of the dragon-man snapped her back to the moment. He was limping towards the edge of the building. In her mind she saw him running up the wall and away from their first fight.

"Let's see how you like it."

She broke into a run. Neko Mata was looking over the railing when she made contact. Part of the stone wall meant to protect people and keep them from falling shattered as Pussy ran through it, taking him with her.

And then they were falling.

Pussy had been here before, but not like this. The first time she was near the wall. Now she and the dragon were falling away. Below them was nothing but trees and parking lot. And it was fast approaching.

His claws dragged across her back again and again. The desperate flailing of a man realizing his doom.

Eighteen stories. Four or five seconds. It was plenty of time for Pussy. The Fizz changed her perceptions. The ground was far away, but the tree was going to be close enough to reach. With a little help, anyway.

Her feet pulled up under her, and she pushed off Neko Mata, separating them slightly. Those few inches were all she needed.

Her hand hit the first branch and bounced off. The second and third branches cracked and split with a thunderous sound as she impacted them. Her left hand found a grip on the fourth limb, even as the protruding growth on it pierced her palm and exited the back of her hand.

She came to a stop. Not a slow easy stop, but a sudden, jarring end to her fall. A sharp popping sound emanated from her shoulder, and she hung like a rag doll on a clothesline.

The thunderous crash below her blotted out any other sound she might have noticed. Instinctively, she threw her right hand up to grab hold beside the left. The pain in her shoulder took over and she almost cried out as she tried to pull herself onto the limb. Instead, she just hung there.

She looked down. It was still a good fifty feet to the ground. It was going to hurt to go the rest of that distance. Not as badly as it hurt Neko Mata, though.

The car he impacted was ruined. The roof was caved in, and at least one of the tires burst from the impact. His body lay twisted among the metal. An odd sculpture of flesh and steel telling a story of destruction.

And then he moved. She had to blink a couple of times to make sure, but his arm was moving. And then a leg. It wasn't quick, but it was obvious that he was trying to pull himself out of the wreckage.

Pussy ground her teeth together. "I don't think so, pal."

She let go of the limb. In the scant second it took to reach the ground, Pussy managed to twist her body and aim carefully.

Her legs caught the majority of the impact against the already-ruined vehicle, but it was her fist that carried her momentum. All the power she had in her arms merged with the energy of the fall. She put every ounce of it into a single punch to the monster's chest.

The bones cracked upon impact. Some from him, and some from her. They weren't alone. The remaining tires exploded. The wheels snapped off. The body of the car fell directly against the tarmac.

She didn't move. His chest rose and fell beneath her fist, but just barely. A gurgle accompanied every breath from the dragon beneath her, and he made no further attempt to move.

That's when her body gave out. She tumbled off of him, falling out of the remains of the car and onto the road beneath.

The street should have felt cold. The sun had been down for a good while, and under these trees it never heated up that much. So, it should have been cold. She didn't feel cold. She couldn't feel anything.

Noises approached. One direction seemed a little more distinct than the others. Someone touched her. She didn't argue.

The noises sharpened. Like daggers they turned from a buzz to piercing sounds. Loud crying sounds. A siren. It was a siren.

"Let's get the board under her. We gotta get her to the hospital." He was definitely upset. She wanted to calm him down.

She raised her head. "Are you okay?"

"Good gravy!" He shouted. "You need to lie back down. We've got to get you to a hospital."

"No, don't worry." She saw his catlike reflexes already assessing her situation. "I'm actually okay. Just had the wind knocked out of me."

"Lady, you fell off a building. You don't get the wind knocked out of you from that." His hands were on her again, urging her to lie down.

The attempt to raise her hand up met with resistance. Most notably the fact that her arm wouldn't move. "I think you might be right. My shoulder has popped out of the socket. Can you put it back?"

"Put it…? I have no idea how you are even talking. That other guy…."

Other guy? Neko Mata. She turned her head. The dragon was gone. In its place was a white feline with twin tails.

"Be careful with him," she stated. "He needs to go to jail."

"He's going to the hospital. If he survives, the cops can come drag him to the lock up." The medic eased her to a standing position. "If I can't get you to the hospital, will you at least let me examine you? I'd like to bandage up that hand if nothing else."

What did he say? She looked at her hand. Blood covered the entire thing. And there was some evidence of a hole running through the palm and out the back.

"Sure." Pussy nodded. Everything was coming back into focus. "The penthouse. Has anybody…?"

"There are people up there already. Don't worry about them. Let's just worry about you." He led her slowly over toward his ambulance.

"Fair enough." It was best to give him the benefit of the doubt.

"Pussy!"

It wasn't the quickest turn, but she angled her head towards George as he came rushing up. "Hi, George. How's things upstairs?"

"A bit of a mess, honestly. But it's a mess that's cleaning up in a good way." He got to them. "What…." He looked up. She followed his gaze to the penthouse balcony.

"Yeah. Long fall," she admitted.

"I didn't know that…. You are on…?" George started a couple of sentences. Both of them had the same question behind them.

"Me either. And yes, I am. That's the reason I'm okay." She looked at the medic. He was tending to her hand. "And okay might be a strong term. I'll be fine in a couple hours. Maybe a couple of days. We'll see. I might want to go have a couple drinks though, just to be safe." Her eyes traveled George's body. "You look like you've been through the ringer, yourself."

"Just contributing." He rubbed his shoulder. "Gonna be a bit sore tomorrow."

"I'm pretty sure I'm going to be sore for a week," she laughed.

"I still think you need to go to the hospital," the medic announced. "That's a nasty wound in your hand. It might need surgery."

"I'll have it looked at, I promise." She gestured to her shoulder with her head. "Now, can I get you to pop that back?"

He was the definition of begrudged agreement at that moment. Grabbing the arm and the shoulder firmly, he hesitated. Three seconds later he simultaneously pushed and pulled on her. She felt the shoulder return to place.

"You are one tough broad," the medic said. "I'd have screamed like a little girl." He looked at the broken car. "Well, I'd be dead, actually."

"Thanks." Pussy winced as she rolled the shoulder once. George's hands were surprisingly soft on her arm as he moved to hold it in place.

"You might want to take it easy with that. At least until it heals." George looked at the medic. "Do you have a sling?"

"Sure. Let me go grab it." He jogged around to the side of the ambulance.

"Now, honestly," George looked in her eyes, "are you okay?"

"I will be. I'm pretty sure I have a dozen or so cracked bones in various places. And my head's still a little scrambled, but everything should heal up fine." His eyes were deep enough to get lost in. She went ahead and took that trip.

"Good. You had me scared." His other hand went up to her face. She felt him brush her hair back. "You look a little scorched, too."

"Play with fire, you know."

"I'm a fireman. I know." He chuckled. She did, too.

"Okay, let me get that arm in a sling." The medic was back and just as focused as before. "Hold her arm for just one more minute."

He went to work. She ignored him. Out of the corner of her eye she saw someone else being rolled out of the building.

Detective Lila Ringtail. She was in a wheelchair.

"What happened to Detective Ringtail?" She nodded her way. "She okay?"

"Bad cut on her leg. Didn't hit any major arteries, though. She should be fine."

"Can she walk?" Pussy asked.

"Probably, but it's not the best idea. Why?"

Pussy felt her jaw clench. "We're not done. I need her help. And we've got to do it tonight. There's still a killer to catch."

Chapter Twenty-Three

Time and weather had not been kind to the mailbox. It looked as though a strong wind or a curious bird could topple it and send the old thing to its doom. Despite that, she could clearly read the numbers painted on the side. Eight. Three. Seven.

Part of her said that she should knock. Give the benefit of the doubt. Common sense told her better. The door didn't want to open, but she lifted and pushed at the same time, and it gave way. It made enough noise to wake the dead, but it opened.

"So much for surprise," Pussy mumbled.

The outside looked worn. The inside showed signs of life. The smell of food hit her. Something exotic and spicy. It wasn't a fresh smell, but rather the memory of a recently eaten dinner.

The only light in the room came through the windows. The moon was bright and cast the world in a bluish tint. No details showed themselves, but if needed, she brought a flashlight for that purpose.

A noise broke through the darkness. The sound of something, or someone, scurrying across the floor in the next room.

Pussy eased that room's door open. She could make out the vague shapes in the darkness, but no details. The three of them huddled in the corner, holding each other for support. Or warmth.

The flashlight revealed them. Three women, each one naked. Chains tied their wrists and ankles. Just tight enough to keep them from running or fighting back.

"It's all right," Pussy whispered. "I'm not going to hurt you."

They were striking. Unique and exotic for this part of the world. A feline, but with a flat face and longer fur. Persian by descent. The one beside her was even more particular. Pussy didn't know the exact origin of her kind, but she looked descended from the deer family. If that deer had a longer face with protracted horns and curving black markings on her face. Both of them stared with wide eyes. And they peeked out from behind a much larger woman. A pure white ursine whose eyes seemed as black as the night itself. She held herself forward, protecting the others.

"None of you understand me, do you?" Pussy asked softly. "You have no idea what's happening to you."

The foremost woman's face scowled, but some of the fear and anger left. The other two had their hands on her back, ready to duck behind her if needed.

Something pressed into Pussy's back.

"You shouldn't have come here."

She didn't move. The point of the knife was easy to identify. And the person wielding it had it positioned well.

"What should I have done? Did you think that I wouldn't come looking for you?" Pussy asked.

"Put your hands behind you."

Pussy obliged. Her flashlight was pulled from her hand. The click of the handcuffs closing matched how tight they felt on her wrists. A hand grabbed her by the shoulder and spun her around.

"You shouldn't have come here!"

The flashlight was set on a nearby table. The glow filled the room like a dying flame. Pussy looked at the knife glinting in the dim light. Then to the face of the woman wielding it. "What are you going to do? Are you going to kill me, too?"

"I…no. No, I won't."

A fire burned deep inside Pussy, quenched by the icy feeling she swallowed.

"Why? Just tell me why, Coney!" Pussy fought to hold back tears.

Her friend stood there, staring at her blankly. "You don't know, Pussy. You couldn't know."

"Then why didn't you tell me!" Pussy shouted. "Was the trip to the club just to get me involved? Did you need a patsy? A fall girl? Was that all just to get me to come looking for you the next day?"

"Not entirely, no." Coney shook her head. "I did want to see you. I wanted to…." She swallowed down the next words. "Someone was going to have to identify my body. You were the only one who could. I didn't expect you to come looking for me like that."

"Who was she? The girl I mean. The one you killed." Pussy felt her shoulders tighten up.

"Does it matter?" Coney replied.

"Of course it does!" Pussy growled. "You killed someone, Coney!"

"I had to! You don't know, Pussy. You couldn't know." A crack appeared in Coney's voice. "You never had to worry about your next meal. Whether or not you were going to wake up the next morning. It was a nightmare."

"I lived that life alongside you. You know what happened to me. I wasn't in any—"

"Not here!" Coney interrupted. "Overseas. It was hard. I got lost and had no way to get home or even let anyone know. And then Drago stepped in and offered me everything." She spit on the ground. "Everything but my freedom."

Coney lowered the knife. The flashlight stayed on the table, casting a long shadow as she began to pace.

"I worked my way up the ladder. Became a trusted worker for him. Waiting. Planning. There was just no way to get out. He would find me." Coney began to rub her left hand with her right. "When the chance came, I had to take it. I had to."

"What happened, Coney? Tell me. Please," Pussy pleaded.

Coney stopped pacing. She stared at Pussy. Their eyes met, but Pussy only saw blackness in the faded light.

"Someone contacted me. Found me somehow." Coney's voice went distant. "I never knew. How could I? But when she sent the letter saying she was my sister, I couldn't believe it."

"Sister?" Pussy whispered. "You're an orphan."

"That doesn't mean I couldn't have a sister. Technically, half sister, really. Same father. Different mothers," Coney explained.

"But the resemblance…. You saw it. She sent a photo. She looked so much like me. It got me thinking. It was a way out. Everything could work."

She started pacing again. "So, I put the pieces together. I had to escort these girls here. I told her we should meet up. It wasn't enough to just disappear. I had to be gone. For good. And I needed him to chase after me, so," Coney stopped and pointed to the room behind Pussy, "I stole them. I knew Drago would be furious."

The pacing resumed. "I had to time things. Make it all work. I contacted Drago. Pretended to be scared and sorry. Told him to come meet me. I invited Tracy—that was my sister's name, Tracy—I told her to come earlier that same day. She was so excited to meet me." Coney's lip twitched. "I hated having to poison her. She seemed so nice."

Pussy picked up the story for her. "She wasn't a perfect match, though. So you beat her. Once the poison started taking effect, she couldn't fight back. You bruised her enough to hide any differences." The images from the apartment replayed inside Pussy's head. "You were hoping Drago would come. You wanted me to find him over your body, not that…not Neko."

"I didn't want you to find anyone. That's where things went wrong," Coney explained. "You weren't supposed to be there at all. I called the police when I saw Neko arrive. They were supposed to catch him, not you."

"She didn't answer the door. You left the front door unlocked. He got there and locked it behind him, after he found her on the floor." Pussy's eyes narrowed. "She wasn't dead when I got there. If I hadn't shown up he would have torn her to pieces. He was going to torture that girl. Because of you. You did that."

"I didn't! She was my way out. My only hope. I didn't want to hurt her at all. I didn't have a choice." There was a pleading in Coney's voice.

"A choice? You killed her!" Pussy lurched forward. Coney raised the knife again. "And you always had a choice. You came to see me the night before. I could have helped you. All you had to do was ask."

"No! I wasn't going to get you hurt. I had to do this. Me! Alone! I was going to do something this time! Without you. Without anyone!" Coney screamed.

"What? Coney, do you know how much I looked up to you? How much you taught me?" The cracks in Pussy's voice threatened to betray her. "You've already done so much."

"That's not true!" Coney protested. "Besides, you were…you've always been better off than me."

Pussy shook her head. "No. I'm not better than anyone. I'm just willing to fight to the end, no matter what."

"Sure, but you've got that…that drink. The thing that makes you better." Coney nodded. "Oh yeah. You told me about it one night. We were both drunk, but I remembered."

"Then you know I could have helped!" Pussy took another step. "I would have done anything for you, Coney."

"Then why did you come looking for me?" Coney took a step closer herself. "And how did you find me, anyway? What gave me away?"

"You weren't as clever as you thought," Pussy said. "Too many things didn't fit together. Someone suggested that I get my head ripped off. It struck me that Neko should have torn the body apart in a fight. There were no cuts at all in her skin. It left doubt in my mind. And then there was this," Pussy pulled a chain from her sleeve. She turned around and dropped the necklace on the table. "This is yours. You always wore this. Always. Even when you showered. So, why wasn't it around your neck? Why would you suddenly be holding it? Why was it in your hand? Why was it in her hand?"

"I…I gave it to her. She saw it on me and said she wanted one of her own. Something to bind us together. As sisters," Coney whispered. "It helped me gain her trust. I think that she really liked it."

"I have no doubt about that. I saw her eyes as she died, Coney. There wasn't anger or fear. There was just pain. She felt betrayed. I swore to find her killer. No matter what." Pussy took a deep breath. "And the Fizz. I don't know how much I told you, but it also gives me visions. Not of things from the past, but the future. And I saw you, Coney. I knew you were alive. The final confirmation came when I had a friend look at the…at your sister's body. You hide the spot on your face with makeup that lasts for days. It was clear as day when I saw your sister. It was hidden the night before, so why was it visible now? He checked it. She had a spot, but it wasn't the same as yours. You had to fix it with makeup. He confirmed that for me, and I knew for certain. I knew you were alive."

Pussy glanced around her. "As to this place, you always talked about it. Many times you said that it was the only thing you liked from your time at the orphanage. You told me about them bringing you kids up here once a year for a getaway. You called it 'eighty-third and seven.' It wasn't too hard to track once I remembered that part."

Coney stood in silence. The deep shadows from the flashlight sank the features of her face. "You were always too smart, Pussy. Too good. I could never compare to you. It's why I left. I couldn't live in your shadow anymore."

"There was never a shadow," Pussy countered. "You were my best friend. I looked up to you. I wanted both of us to be the same. Have the same opportunities and future. I would have shared everything with you."

"Shared!" Coney laughed. "That's just it. You got it all. I got the scraps. Maybe sometimes I didn't want the scraps! Did you ever think of that? It's possible that Coney—poor, CUTE little Coney—could do some things for herself!"

"Not this way." Pussy glanced over her shoulder. "What about them? Why are they here?"

"I'm going to sell them." Ice shivered through Pussy's veins, brought about by the frozen tone of Coney's voice. "I know all of Drago's buyers. These three are rare. I can get enough money to go away and start my own life."

"They're people, not product." Pussy stood up tall. "And no, you aren't going to sell them."

"You don't have control here, Pussy!" Light flashed off of the knife's blade. "I do!"

The sharp sound of metal snapping caused Coney to jump. As Pussy moved her hands back in front of her, she saw realization sink into Coney's face.

"No, Coney, you don't." Pussy held out her hand. "Give me the knife. End this peacefully. Please."

Coney's whole body lurched with every breath. Her eyes couldn't move from the fractured handcuffs. "How did you…?"

"I apparently didn't tell you everything about Fizz." She took a step closer. "Please."

"I'm not going back to him," Coney said. "I can't. I won't."

"Drago is in jail. He'll be there for a long time. Neko and Tayra, as well. They won't get you. They can't get you." With the touch of a loved one, Pussy took hold of Coney's hand. The knife came out easily. "I'm sorry. You have no idea how sorry I am."

"Can't you…." A tear filled Coney's eye. "Please, Pussy. Let me go. I've been…. You don't know."

"You're right, I don't." Pussy put her arm around Coney and started towards the door. "I never will. But no, I can't let you go." She looked down at Coney. The tears fell in streaks. "I can see how it changed you. What Drago did to you. The Coney I knew couldn't have done anything like this. She was kind and gentle. You killed someone. I can't ignore that."

The door stood open. A pair of figures waited in the darkness beyond it. The bright spot of a burning cigarette was in the mouth of one.

"Coney Hase," Detective Ringtail stepped towards them, "you're under arrest for murder."

Officer Stye moved towards Coney. She looked up at Pussy again.

"I'm scared." It wasn't a voice that Pussy recognized.

"I know. I am, too. I just wish you had told me that at the beginning." She held onto Coney's hand until it was time to let go.

Epilogue

Two bottles rested on the table. The bottle with the brown liquid was only half full. The label on it was fresh, and the cap rested next to it. The bottle containing the red liquid barely had enough to qualify as a shot.

The glass in front of her was empty.

"Hey, Pussy?" Robby's voice was soft and warm. "Can I get you something to eat? You're probably hungry, right?"

She shook her head. "I'm fine, Robby."

Despite staring at the glass in front of her, she could still see him. No. Not see him. She felt him. Hovering over her. "I said I'm fine, Robby."

He pulled the chair out like it was a thorn in his hand. She finally looked at him when he sat across from her. "All due respect, Boss, no, you ain't. You're about as far from fine as I've ever seen you."

"Okay, you're right." Pussy agreed. "I should say that I'll be fine."

"I'm not so sure. This shook you up. Bad." Robby leaned in towards the table. "You've been sitting here all day, just drinking that stuff. I have no idea how you aren't drunk off your mind."

"It's what I do," she laughed. "I drink this stuff."

"No it ain't. Look, I dunno what happened, but you ain't the type of dame who does this." He reached for the bottle. Her hand was quicker.

"Not that one." She pushed the bottle of whiskey closer to him.

He took it and set it on the floor beside him. "Pussy, you got friends, y'know. Everybody here is one."

"Actually, no." The chair groaned as she leaned back. "Everyone here is family. I've learned a valuable lesson in the past few days. Something that I knew all along. Friends are fleeting. Family is forever."

He smiled at her. It was nice. It took her a moment to realize that he was just responding to the expression on her face.

"Let me get you some food." He stood up from the chair. "Please?"

"Miss Katnip?" There was a hesitation in Robin's voice. "You have a visitor."

She and Robby turned as one. Robin stood next to an exotic looking woman with dark fur and eyes of piercing blue.

"Food later." She stood up from the table. "Robby, I want you to meet someone."

The woman fidgeted as they approached. "Robby, may I introduce Desiree. She's the new bartender."

"What?" She didn't need to look his way to see Robby's expression.

"I figured you could use some help. She'll be working with you. You're the lead bartender, but," Pussy pointed to Desiree, "I'd listen to what she has to say. I've never met anyone with her kind of talent."

"Oh! Okay, yeah. I can show the kid what's what." He stuck a hand towards her. "Name's Robby. Good t'meet you."

"Thank you, Mr. Robby." Desiree took his hand and bowed her head. "I will do what I can to make you proud."

"Yeah, uh, okay." His eyes were a little glazed over. Pussy did what she could not to laugh. She couldn't push down the giggle.

"And to you, Miss Pussy Katnip." Desiree let go of his hand and bowed at the waist towards her. "I am forever in your debt."

The words sank into Pussy's flesh like daggers. She put her hand on Desiree's chin and lifted it gently. "No, you aren't. You have a job here. And you will have it for as long as you like. But you are not in my debt. You're free."

The white of Desiree's teeth against the black of her face lit up the room. "Thank you, ma'am. I will do you proud, as well."

"I have no doubt." She pointed towards the bar. "Why don't you show her around, Robby."

"My pleasure." He stepped to the side. "C'mon, Desiree. I'll show you the ropes."

"Ropes?" Her face twisted. "Why do you use ropes?"

"I…." He looked at Pussy. Several thoughts crossed her mind, but she chose to shrug. He turned back to Desiree. "Just c'mon."

Pussy watched them walk away. His bright red and her rich black were a striking contrast. Like a rose in the night. "That should be good for business," she mumbled.

"She's pretty," Robin said. "Where did you meet her?"

"She poured me a drink the other night," Pussy said.

"That must have been a heck of a drink." The light shifted in Robin's eyes, showing curiosity and disbelief in equal measure.

"It was a good drink." Pussy put her hand on Robin's shoulder. "And she needed someone. She's alone here. I couldn't just abandon her. You understand."

"Yeah. I got you, Miss Katnip. Besides, she seems nice. And really, really pretty." The expression on Robin's face went from curiosity to curious.

"Is this a bad time?"

"Not at all." Pussy turned towards their new guest. "Thank you for coming down."

Lila leaned heavily on a cane to her left side. The bulge under her pant leg hinted at the bandages lying beneath. "It's the least I can do. How are you feeling?"

"I'm fine. How's the leg?" Pussy stepped over towards her.

"It hurts. Almost like someone cut it deep. That's okay. I only use it every alternate step." Her eyes ran up and down Pussy. "And you're looking…fine. So, you gonna tell me how it is that you're okay after falling off an eighteen story building?"

"Just lucky, I guess." Pussy motioned to her table.

Lila limped towards it. "So, that's a no, then." She pushed the chair out and didn't sit as much as fall into the seat. "You do know it's my job to find out secrets, right?"

"I have nothing to hide, Detective." Pussy sat across from her.

"I'm pretty sure that every person I've ever spoken to has said that same thing." She pulled the cigarette from her mouth and tapped the ashes off into the nearby ashtray.

"I wanted to thank you for clearing my name. It might have been impossible without your help," Pussy stated.

"You're welcome. I think I could say the same thing about finding the moles in the force." Lila glanced down. Her hand disappeared and came back holding a bottle of whiskey. "Do you always keep your booze on the floor?"

"Have you been able to root out everyone who was on the take?" Pussy redirected.

"Not everyone. Some of the cops we found evidence against in Drago's books show up clean. Not a shred of evidence on their side to match them getting a bribe." She put the bottle on the table and pulled out the cork. "It's their word against some crooked books. Not gonna be easy."

Lila poured a good shot into the empty glass in front of Pussy.

"At least you have a list. It's a start." Pussy picked up the glass and held it high. Lila did the same with the bottle.

Pussy emptied her glass. Lila turned the bottle straight up.

"Whew!" Lila shook her head and put the bottle on the table. "That stuff is a little rough straight."

"Not much of a drinker?" Pussy asked.

Lila simply smiled.

"What about Drago?" Pussy saw no need to pursue the other matter. "And his flunkies for that matter?"

"That Neko fella got some protection from his country. They flew him out of here yesterday. Something about a diplomatic controversy, I think." Lila took a deep drag from her cigarette. "Tayra isn't as lucky. He's gonna be behind bars for a good while. Drago," she rolled her eyes, "he's fighting it, of course. Hired some fancy lawyer. Far as I'm concerned he hasn't got a shot, but that isn't my job."

"He belongs under the jail," Pussy growled. "Were you able to get any of the other people he was keeping back to their homes?"

"Some. Most, actually. There are still a couple that haven't left." Lila's eyes drifted towards the bar. "I guess you already knew that, though."

"Desiree is here by choice, Detective. You can ask her yourself." Pussy leaned forward.

"I'm not worried. You aren't that type."

"What about Coney?" Pussy asked. "Is there any chance that she…?"

"That she what? The woman admitted to murder and to a plot to sell three innocent women as slaves. Everything is cut and dried there," Lila stated.

"I imagine." The breath Pussy took in seemed to take forever. "It probably sounds stupid to say, but I'm worried about her. I can't help it."

"It's not stupid," Lila answered. "Just don't let it get to you." She tapped the bottle of whiskey. "You won't find answers here."

"I know. I just wished it helped me to forget. Unfortunately, I've got something of a strong constitution. Whiskey doesn't work on me much anymore."

"Somehow, I'm not surprised." She pointed at the bottle next to Pussy. "I'm curious what that is, though."

"This?" Pussy held up the bottle of Fizz. It's contents swirled shades of red in the bottom of the decanter. "An old family recipe. I'd offer you a taste, but the last person who sampled it had a bad reaction. I'd rather not go through that again."

"I imagine not."

The sounds of the bar grew louder. Or perhaps it was just the lack of conversation at the table.

"Still not gonna tell me, huh?" Lila asked.

"I have no idea what you're talking about," Pussy answered.

"You punched a dragon. Fell off a building. Who knows what else?" Her eyes wandered over Pussy again. "And you look fresh as the morning."

"Good genes." Pussy smiled across the table.

"Uh-huh."

"I was also wondering if you could do me a favor." Pussy pushed the bottle off to the side. "The bar across the street— the Dogg House—is run by someone who isn't always on the up and up."

"Okay," Lila responded. "Is there something you know he's doing?"

"Oh, no. Nothing at the moment," Pussy chuckled. "I normally keep a fairly close eye on him, too. But in exchange for some information, I promised to ignore him for a while. I'm not the type to break a promise. I was hoping you might be able to look in on him from time to time."

"You never know. Anonymous tips happen all the time." Lila crushed out her cigarette and immediately pulled out a new one. It was lit before she started the next sentence. "I think that he can have some officers visiting his place for a while."

"Thank you. I don't like to see bad things happen and sit on my hands." Pussy smiled.

"I picked that up about you," Lila said. "Is that all you need?"

"That pretty much covers everything," Pussy answered.

Lila moved her cane out to one side and pushed against it. Her leg threatened to betray her and send her tumbling, but she rose to a standing position. "I guess I'll be going then."

Pussy joined her and walked towards the door. "Well, thank you again for coming by."

"My pleasure," Lila replied.

"Oh, Detective," Pussy stepped in front of Lila, forcing the officer to stop, "there is one other thing."

Lila raised an eyebrow. Their eyes met.

"What are your intentions with George?" There was gravel in Pussy's voice.

"I beg your pardon?" The edge in Lila's voice whet against that gravel.

"You heard me."

Lila pulled the cigarette from her mouth. A dense cloud of smoke surrounded Pussy's head.

"George is a grown man, Miss Katnip. He can go—or do—as he chooses."

"Yes he is, and yes he can." Pussy parted through the fog. "I just prefer you not encourage him down the wrong path."

"The wrong path? Is that a threat, Miss Katnip?" Lila snarled.

"Not at all. I would never threaten a police officer." Pussy raised her head up. "We're on the same side, after all."

"Are we, now?" Lila answered.

"Definitely. You see, I've known George for a long time. We're very close. There is a bond we share. I'd hate to see something—or someone—come between us." Pussy's tongue played across her fangs.

"Really? That's interesting. How well do you know him?" Lila asked. "For example, do you know what side of the bed he likes to sleep on?" The detective's eyes burned. "Because I do."

Pussy heard a heartbeat. Maybe two.

"I think this conversation is over," Pussy growled.

"Don't count on it." Lila snapped right back at her.

"You know the way out." She stepped to one side, leaving a clear path for Detective Ringtail.

Lila stood there for a second. Pussy watched the wheels turning behind her eyes. "Have a good day, Miss Katnip."

"And you as well, Detective."

The detective walked past her. Pussy didn't bother to turn around. She walked back towards the bar. In the distance she heard the front door close.

"All right, everyone, listen up." The room turned at the sound of her voice. All the employees from across the club gathered around. A dozen eyes looked at her. Each pair belonging to someone unique. Someone special. "The Kit Kat Klub isn't just a place. It's a feeling. A sensation of having one moment in life where everything is good. That whatever pain you are feeling outside can't reach you in here. You're safe from the evil and misery that's been hunting you down. Guests are counting on us, whether we know it or not. We need to be people doing what we can to make sure they aren't disappointed. I know you are those people. The right people."

Pussy Katnip went to the table and picked up the bottle of Fizz. "Let's get to work."

THE END

Afterword

I certainly hope you enjoyed *The Devil Was Green*. This is the second novel in the Pussy Katnip series, but will certainly not be the last one. In fact, the next chapter of her saga is in *A Touch of Gold*, a new short story available on Amazon.com.

As always, though, we rely upon you to help things continue. Word of mouth is the best advertisement that we can get, and anything that you can do to help us out will keep Pussy and her stories coming back again and again.

So, leave a review on Amazon or Goodreads. Tell a friend. Share your opinion on social media. That's the lifeblood of books like this one. Let's keep Pussy Katnip alive for a long time.

And if you get a chance, sign up for my mailing list at publishing.pandahead.com. I'll give you a free original short story just for signing up.

Thanks for reading. See you again soon.

> *- Brett Brooks*

www.ingramcontent.com/pod-product-compliance
Lightning Source LLC
Chambersburg PA
CBHW060522260626
47161CB00003B/727